Leather and Grit

WRESTLING
WITH DESTINY

JON KEYS

Wrestling with Destiny
ISBN # 978-1-83943-802-8
©Copyright Jon Keys 2018
Cover Art by Erin Dameron-Hill ©Copyright April 2018
Interior text design by Claire Siemaszkiewicz
Pride Publishing

Pride Publishing books by Jon Keys

Single Books
Showstring
Crossfire
Tackling the Subject
A Matter of Priority
Construction

Leather and Grit
Drawing the Devil
Wrestling with Destiny
Roping in his Heart

Anthologies
Right Here, Right Now: Throwaway

WRESTLING
WITH DESTINY

Chapter One

Tyler struggled to settle his nerves. This was the biggest rodeo he'd participated in since graduating from college and deciding to go for the National Finals. It wasn't a choice he'd made lightly, but the state-of-the-art rig his mother had given him when he'd graduated had made the decision easier. *It's a sweet setup for Rusty and I both.*

As if his horse knew that thoughts of him passed through Tyler's mind, Rusty pressed against his owner, and with great care, put his hoof on top of Tyler's boot and leaned toward the cowboy.

Tyler yelped and shoved on the big gelding. "Damn you! Get off my foot! Ahh!"

Everett chuckled. As Tyler's hazer, he kept the steer from running the wrong direction while Tyler jumped from his horse. Close to ten years older than Tyler, Everett had only worked with him since the start of the season. Tyler didn't have the option of continuing to compete with his college partner. Chuck had two more years before he'd graduate and his father had made it very clear that if Tyler talked his son into quitting school, he'd beat Tyler like a drum.

Tyler had seen it as a serious threat and made sure to discourage any ideas Chuck'd had along those lines. His college rodeo coach had suggested Everett. While not the most congenial partner on the tour, he did his job well. Just as important, Tyler being gay hadn't seemed to be an issue.

Rusty shifted his weight enough for Tyler to jerk his foot out, and Everett commented, "You've let that animal think for himself far too much. He'll dump you one of these days."

Tyler laughed at the idea as he did his usual pre-run check of his equipment. The horse behaved while Tyler tugged the cinch tight. But on his second pull, an ominous pop filled the room.

"What the hell?"

Tyler ran his hands along both sides of the strap. When the first pass found nothing, he calmed himself enough to give the strap a more detailed evaluation.

There it is, past the buckle. A weak spot.

"Something's wrong with the saddle. I'll be back in a sec," he told Everett as he led his mount out of the holding pen. He moved at a fast walk until they'd cleared the crowd then dropped into a sprint toward the trailer. His spare tack supply was extensive, and it only took a few minutes to replace it.

He untied the horse, swung into the saddle and urged Rusty into a gallop. He slowed when he neared the entry, but his rapid pace still earned him a paint-peeling glare from the guy serving as gateman. He brought Rusty to a stop at Everett's flank, and his hazer turned with a raised eyebrow. "I started to think we were giving up."

Tyler shifted back and forth until he knew the new equipment was in good shape. He finished as they were called to the arena. He rode Rusty to the left-side box that had seen more than its share of wear over the decades and his horse banged into it a few times as the excitement grew. Tyler settled the gelding into the box's far corner, and once every detail satisfied him, he nodded for the steer's release.

The rangy red-and-white-mottled animal shot through the open space like a West Texas jackrabbit. But Tyler had dealt with animals similar to this daily for the last ten years.

Already straining to close the interval, he urged Rusty to the short-distance speed bred into the quarter horse. A second later they raced beside the steer. Tyler made all the last second changes and urged a burst of speed from his mount before launching himself.

Tyler equated the instant of weightlessness when he was off his mount to an eagle soaring above its prey. In his mind, the flight lasted less than a thump of his pounding heart. His fantasy burst when he landed on the animal and slammed to the reality of sweat, dirt and racing beef.

He curled his muscular arm around one of its short, thick horns. The other arm snaked its way to the muzzle and Tyler dug his boots into the dry powder under them.

Focused on a single task, he torqued his body, bringing into use every muscle developed over the years. When he twisted the animal around, there was an instant when everything froze in place as the final scene of the drama unfolded with the two gladiators straining to defeat each other.

With a final effort, Tyler won the battle and the steer rolled to its back. An instant later, the crowd erupted in a roar as the judge declared his run ended.

He released the steer, climbed to his feet and used his hat to knock off some of the dust covering his body. He smiled when Everett rode close and held out Rusty's reins. "Good run, kid. Your luck is holding."

Tyler listened as the emcee announced his time. Afterward, he turned to Everett with a broad smile. "Four-point-eight. I'm feeling like a winner tonight." He mounted Rusty to follow Everett to the staging pens then to their trailers. Everett unsaddled his own horse and had her loaded almost before Tyler dismounted. He locked his trailer shut and flashed Tyler a wave. "Later. See ya next weekend."

Before Tyler could do more than return the wave, Everett had left the fairground and disappeared behind a boiling cloud of dust. He waited for the clue to gaining a better understanding of his hazer and his lack of warmth, but after considering it for a few seconds, he shook his head at the reoccurring issue. Tyler considered himself good at making people feel comfortable, but his skill seemed to be ineffective with Everett. Knowing he might never understand the man, he turned to unsaddle Rusty. He was in no particular rush. His next destination was home and nothing urged him to hurry his return.

He tugged off his saddle and tossed it onto a rack. He brushed Rusty until the horse leaned into each stroke then loaded him into the trailer and used the last of the evening sun to see if he could tell what had happened to his original saddle. He tugged the damaged tack into the light and checked the leather inch-by-inch but revealed nothing new. The front cinch had developed a thin crease that weakened with each movement.

He leaned against the trailer and laughed when a dark red muzzle appeared. Tyler scratched the horse's nose as he tried to figure out why the weakness had developed in the cinch. With a final sigh, he pushed off the trailer and readied everything for their trip home. He didn't have a clue what was causing the issue with his equipment but he knew its investigation couldn't be delayed for long.

* * * *

Micah drove the utility vehicle into the welcome shade of the tool shed and sighed. *What a long day.* He was making progress on the fence replacement, but on some days, it felt as if his progress could be measured in inches. He stared at the leather gloves that were becoming flayed from the miles of barbed wire redone so far this spring. But, in reality, he had been productive. Today he'd managed to finish an entire section of fencing, giving Micah a sense of accomplishment on what seemed to be a never-ending task of keeping the ranch operational. As he unloaded the tools and materials from the job, the two blue heelers who were the working dogs for their ranch threw themselves into the shade. He reached down to give each of them a loving scratch behind their ears. "Get some rest, guys. You were good company this afternoon, but we have a lot more to go this summer." Smiling at the familiar interaction, he turned back to his work.

"How'd it go this afternoon?"

Micah sighed at hearing his father's voice. He put the fencing pliers onto the pegboard and turned to his dad. "Good. Got a lot done. I finished repairing the section of fence that butts up against the old Parker place. Everything should be finished this summer. I need to stop by the Lang ranch and talk to them. I want to confirm they'll be willing to help with the shared fencing."

His father chuckled. "Mary Lou won't let you anywhere close to her precious horses with your barbed wire."

He shook his head. "I ran into Lee in the feed store the other day. We'll do vinyl fencing, so there shouldn't be any issues."

"Isn't the Lang boy back from college?"

Micah hesitated to say anything. His dad was too good at reading his thoughts and his infatuation with Tyler Lang was a secret he would prefer to keep to himself. Tyler's muscular body had provided Micah with jack-off fantasies since they'd been in high school. Now his fantasy man was one of the highest-ranked steer wrestlers in the country. There was no way any of those daydreams would come to life. Besides, he couldn't bear the thought of how his dad would react if Micah came out as gay. He couldn't see it happening.

"Micah? Everything okay?"

He dropped the pointless speculation and answered the question. "Someone told me he was back in town. They said he is Grand Marshall for the Fourth of July parade, but I haven't seen him."

His dad frowned. "You work too hard. Take some time off and enjoy yourself. You don't have to finish all the things on your list every day."

Micah made a final check that he'd put everything into its place before turning to his father. "Well, if it will make you feel any better, I planned to go to the rodeo tonight. Dustin Lewis is one of the bull riders. From what I've seen, he's doing better this year. He has a good chance of winning at Nationals."

"Isn't that the boy who's married to another man?"

Micah swallowed hard. "Yeah, he's with Shane Rees, the bullfighter. I don't know if they're married or not."

It was impossible for Micah to interpret his father's expression, but he seemed to be thinking about the information. Then he turned to Micah. "Good. I hope you enjoy yourself. You've earned a break from all the work. Go clean up. I'll feed and water the stock." He waved his hand at Micah as his grin got even larger. "If you don't make it home before dawn, I'll take care of everything then, too."

Micah snorted. "Yeah, like that would ever happen. I'll take care of the animals in the morning. But if you'd do the evening feeding, I wouldn't mind getting to the fairground in time to see everything before the rodeo begins."

He waved Micah toward the house. "Go get ready. I can handle a few old hens and a lazy bull."

"Thanks, Dad. I'll tell you all about it tomorrow."

A short time later, Micah sat on the bench in the entryway, pulling off his boots before moving into his room. In the dim, cool bedroom he had no trouble smelling the odor from a day of hard work. He wrinkled his nose as he stripped off the last of his clothing and dropped it all into the hamper. After a relaxing stretch, Micah turned on the shower and adjusted the spray until it was hot enough to begin relaxing his stiff muscles. He stepped inside, the water cascading over his neck, and he moaned. After letting the water wet him thoroughly, Micah soaped himself. He thought about Tyler as his body responded to the fantasy. He teased his soap-covered hand up and down his dick, enjoying the sensation on his now-iron-hard shaft.

Steam filled the glass enclosure as Micah lost himself in the pleasure. He ran his fist up and down his cock as he explored his taut body with his other hand. A minute later, he leaned against the shower wall as he pounded his shaft, his breath coming in gasps. As he tensed with orgasm, he twisted his nipple and sent himself over the edge.

His climax painted the glass door with white lines as he shook with pleasure. With his balls tight against his erupting cock, Micah enjoyed the waves of ecstasy washing over him. He stripped the final strands of cum from his softening dick until he was focused on more than his trembling muscles.

As the last of the sexual euphoria left his body, he stepped back under the cascade to finish his shower. A short time later, he was done and used one of the plush towels to dry himself. He dropped the damp towel into the clothes hamper, walked into the bedroom and went through his closet to look for something to wear. He made his typical choice of pressed Wranglers, a heavy western shirt and boots polished to within an inch of their lives. It was likely he'd run into someone he knew and he planned on being prepared.

Once he had everything in place, including the addition of a tooled leather belt, he checked his appearance in the full-length mirror hanging from the closet door. Satisfied with what he saw, Micah headed out to the fairgrounds.

Chapter Two

Tyler sat relaxed in his saddle as he led the equestrian portion of the Fourth of July parade. His mother had masterminded this whole stunt, and he didn't have a burning desire to be up at ten on a Saturday morning. The hangover from partying with his friends the night before didn't made it any easier. The brilliant sun made his signature sunglasses a vital necessity on this bright day. Even his horse moved as if being up this early was sacrilegious to him, too.

He leaned forward and patted his ride's shoulder. "Hang in there, Rusty. Pretty soon you'll be back in your nice, quiet stall at the ranch, enjoying a feeder full of alfalfa."

There was a soft moan to Tyler's right, and he glanced over. "You doing okay, Everett?"

"Who's the sadistic son-of-a-bitch that schedules these godforsaken parades so early in the morning?"

Tyler grinned as the horses stepped quicker, enjoying the rhythmic sound of their hooves. He didn't mind Everett's grumbling. It kept him from focusing on his own minor discomfort. But he spoke up when he had to dodge the flag Everett carried when his riding partner let it sag.

"Everett! You drop Old Glory and they will be after you with torches and pitchforks. Then it won't matter how early it is."

His hazer snapped the flag back upright with some words muttered under his breath that Micah's Baptist father would be offended to hear. But they continued leading the equestrian group as the parade made its way down Main Street.

Everett perked up and he cut his eyes toward Tyler. "How'd things work out with the cute guy last night? I left with a girl before I knew if you got lucky."

Tyler snorted loud enough that his horse glanced back. "Yeah, things didn't work out too well. The night got a whole lot less interesting after I found out he was jail bait."

"You didn't even swap slobbers with him?"

He glanced at Everett. "There might've been some making out, but he was such a twink that I probably would have broke him if we'd got any more hot and heavy."

Their conversation lapsed for a time as the parade made its way through town. Tyler saw a pack of junior high boys running up and down the route and he got Everett's attention. "Trouble ahead. You better rein in your girl."

Tyler tensed as the tweens moved closer. He couldn't imagine what they might do to bother Rusty, but Everett's pinto mare was a different story. She'd been prancing sideways at every distraction they'd passed so far. Then Tyler's worst-case scenario unfolded when the kids threw lit firecrackers under the horses.

While Rusty gave him the response he expected — a snort at the hooligans — Everett didn't fare as well.

"Shit!" Everett hissed as the horse spun in crazy circles to escape the frightening explosions of gunpowder under her hooves. The miscreants didn't understand the consequences of their devilry, but Tyler could tell Everett's mare was about to lose her crap.

Tyler guided Rusty into the little mob of kids like he would with a group of yearling cattle and cut the leader away from the others. The kid became more frightened each time he turned to escape, only to find himself pinned by Rusty's hindquarters or shoulder. Tyler waited, ready to pounce once the juvenile was overwhelmed by the unflappable horse.

Then it happened. Rusty lunged down with his front hooves inches from the kid. Tyler recognized his opportunity. With one hand in a vise-like grip on the saddle horn, he reached down, grabbed the back of the boy's shirt and hauled him a few feet off the ground. He hung without moving for several seconds before he started to struggle.

"Hey! Let me go. I didn't do anything."

Tyler clenched his fist tighter into the kid's shirt. "I saw you and your buddies throwing firecrackers under the horses. Your stunt might have gotten someone hurt."

He stopped struggling and hung limp from Tyler's hand. "What're you going to do?"

"Can you promise you won't do another stupid stunt like this again?"

About that time, a harried-looking woman made her way through the gathering crowd. She stopped at the edge of the drama and glared at the kid in Tyler's custody. "Kenny, what have you done now?"

Kenny muttered something but Tyler didn't understand what he said.

"Speak up! What'd you do?" the woman asked.

This time his response was loud enough that Tyler heard. "Throwing fireworks. We were just having some fun—"

"Oh, my God! What were you thinking? What if Mr. Lang's horse had spooked? Then someone might have gotten hurt. You owe Mr. Lang compensation for what you did."

Tyler felt a chill run up his spine at the tone of her voice and the implication that Kenny somehow owed him. But the kid was so dejected that Tyler couldn't force himself to run from the situation. He'd been a Big Brother through his last couple of years in college and Kenny's reaction was similar to what he'd found with some of those kids. He studied Kenny's mother and his impression solidified. But if this was going to happen, it would be under Tyler's terms.

"We can work something out, but it requires a commitment from both of you."

From her expression, Tyler knew he had not done what she'd hoped. But if he set the conditions, he could help Kenny without becoming an on-demand sitter.

Tyler lowered Kenny and the boy froze under the gaze locked on him. "You need to understand more about horses. You can come out to the ranch a couple days a week and help. That'll give you enough to keep you busy."

He turned to Kenny's mother. "Drop him off at two and pick him up at five, twice a week. That would be enough for him to learn something."

She gave Tyler a searing glare, took Kenny by the back of his neck and dragged him into the crowd.

Within a few seconds, they had both disappeared down a side street. Everett guided his horse beside Tyler, shaking his head. "That kid's going to be a pain in the ass."

Tyler glanced over with a slight smile. "Maybe. But he reminds me of what hell I dealt everyone until my mom bought the ranch and I fell in love with the horses."

A low snort came from Everett but he didn't comment further as they rejoined the parade. As they made their way down the route, Tyler wondered what kind of mess he'd created for himself. He hoped that some time at the farm would give the boy a unique perspective on life and not a different set of targets for a whole new level of trouble.

* * * *

Micah made his way through the fairgrounds, greeting friends he only saw at similar community events. The county fair remained one of his favorites during the year, and the added excitement of a sanctioned rodeo made it that much better.

But other than the rodeo, he loved to see the FFA and 4-H kids' animals. He grew nostalgic about the time he'd spent working with his cattle and preparing them for the show ring. The variety of types of stock had always been fascinating.

"Hey, Micah, perfect timing. Would you help us clip this heifer?"

Micah glanced over to spot the manager of the Lang ranch, who also was a close friend from high school. In their younger years, he and Lee had spent too many hours to count getting their animals ready until they were groomed better than any dog at the Westminster. The main difference being their animals weighed around a half ton and some of them had no interest in cooperating with humans.

They didn't see each other as often these days. Micah spent all day, every day working, and Lee was not only the manager for the neighboring ranch but also the dad of two little towheaded boys. Those kids were the focus of his problem right now.

"Hey, Lee. It's been years since I've clipped anything."

"Get over here and give us a hand," Lee said.

Micah made his way through the equipment strewn around and to the side of an Angus heifer in the clipping stand. He inspected the calf before turning to Lee and his sons.

"She looks good. What did you need help with?"

Lee said, "I wanted another set of eyes, like we did in high school."

Micah took the clippers and spent a few minutes adjusting the immaculately groomed animal while Lee and his boys watched. Once he'd finished, he handed the clippers back to Lee. "There. That's all I noticed. Otherwise, it's a good job."

Lee turned to his sons. "Take her back to her tie-out spot. She's ready to go."

Once the pair had made their way down the aisle, Lee turned to Micah. "Thanks. They thought their dad was out-of-date. Now they have an expert opinion."

Micah chuckled and shook his head. "I'm so glad we were never that stubborn."

"Yeah, right. Something like that." Lee gave Micah a wink. "What are you doing tonight? Did you come to watch a certain steer wrestler perform?"

Micah's face heated up, but he refused to rise to Lee's bait—even if the crack was true. "I've always liked the fair. We used to be here for every activity when we were old enough. I remember there were other things lost on this fairground, too."

Lee turned crimson and seemed like he was about to pee his pants when Micah continued. "Yup, I understand you lost your house key out here. You told me about losing that key for a long time, too."

Micah chuckled as the color returned to Lee's face. But once he had recovered from Micah's teasing, Lee headed the conversation back in a safer direction. "You going to the rodeo? The competition is pretty stiff since it's sanctioned this year."

"Someone told me that, and the rodeo's part of the reason I came to town. Also…Dad thinks I need a break."

"And stud-boy Tyler's competing, too," Lee said with a snicker.

Micah lifted his eyebrows and ignored the jab. "I haven't seen Tyler since he got a rodeo scholarship and went to Tech."

"Well, he's back and leaving on the rodeo circuit soon. Mary Lou bought him a new truck and trailer as a graduation present. He's entered the steer wrestling tonight." Lee's smile grew. "I understand he's still available, too. You couldn't go for bigger fish than him in this county."

Micah glanced around and was relieved to find no one within hearing distance. "Come on, Lee. You're my best friend and the only person I've told. Give me a break."

"No one's going to care, Micah. It's a different time. It's not like when our daddies were young."

Sadness filled Micah. "I thought things had changed, too. But people are being killed again because they're gay. Things aren't as different as we'd hoped."

The boys reappeared from putting the heifer back, stopping the adults' conversation. Micah focused on the youngsters. "That's a nice heifer, guys. She might win everything."

Ethan, the older of the two, studied Micah then nodded. "Dad helped pick her out. But Austin and I were the ones who made the final decision."

"Well, y'all did a great job. She's one sweet heifer," Micah said.

Ethan moved over to sit on one of their show boxes. Micah watched him relax then turned to Lee. "I think you and the boys have everything under control. I'm going to grab supper and make my way over to the rodeo."

Lee gave him a knowing smile. "Enjoy the scenery."

* * * *

Tyler's nerves flooded with eagerness as the time for his 'go' edged closer. This would be one of his first rodeos since graduation and he was ready to tear into the competitors. Rusty's performance had been outstanding and Tyler expected to win his event tonight. Like always, he'd been visualizing his run. It was his routine for as long as he could remember. But he let his focus drift to other contests. He loved the little kids riding sheep during the mutton-busting competition and it was only one of several events that were too cute to pass up.

Besides thinking it was adorable, Tyler had a vested interest. Lee's two boys were riding tonight. Ethan and

Austin were in the practice pens back home every time he drove past the arena. It was Lee's kids' enthusiasm that got him through training rounds sometimes. But regardless, if they cheered him on, he could do the same for them.

Both boys had done well, and Austin might have ended in the prize money. He'd make certain they both got some kind of reward from him before he left for the next rodeo. But that had been hours ago, and he'd been working himself up to cut off a few critical parts of a second. He'd learned long ago that it took a certain attitude to jump off a galloping horse to catch a steer that weighed twice as much as he did then throw the animal onto its back.

Being full of himself and a little crazy helped.

But after as many years as he'd been at the sport, he had his own method for getting ready. Everett walked his mount as he went through a similar process. After a few slow trips around the exercise pen, Everett rode up beside him and came to a stop. They both focused on the current pair before they spoke to each other.

"You ready for tonight?" Tyler asked.

Everett motioned to him. "My part's easy. All I have to do is keep the steer close enough so you don't fall flat on your face. I've done it for years. It doesn't take much to haze for idiots."

Tyler swung his hat at Everett before popping it back on his head. "I remember a few heated discussions when I'd missed a catch and I told you what I thought of your ancestors."

"Hmm, don't know if I can recall that. Maybe. It's faint these days." He winked at Tyler.

Tyler rolled his eyes but made no comment. As the next dogger missed his steer, Tyler decided there were an abnormal number of bad rides tonight. They sat in quiet contemplation until their run was next. That dogger missed the horns and ended up on his butt in the dust. Tyler twisted his lips as the competitor made his way out of the arena.

Everett eased closer. "He's usually better than that. There's been a lot of missed catches tonight. Too many."

Tyler nodded as he negotiated Rusty into the box. Everett backed his horse into the opposite side. As he readied himself, he spotted an unexpected sight. Kenny was in the front row of the bleachers, watching intently. An instant later, he'd filed the observation away with all the other distractions. His whole focus consisted of having the steer on its back with four feet in the air.

He glanced at Everett and got an almost imperceptible nod. Tyler took a deep breath and signaled.

The world around him transformed into a modern version of the ancient battle between man and beast. The animal burst from the narrow chute at a dead run. At that instant, the horses pounded out of their boxes in pursuit. Within a few massive leaps, Rusty brought Tyler to the distance he needed. He leaned out, dropping the reins while he prepared to jump. As he propelled himself forward, something shifted.

There was a split second when Tyler's world moved out of control. But with his next coherent thought, he recognized the sensation of his arm coming into contact with the steer's left horn. From that point, he fell into a long-developed routine. His heels dug into the arena floor as Tyler twisted the muscular calf downward.

He strained for the needed muscle that put the steer on its back with all four hooves in the air. Once Tyler released the animal, it popped to its feet and dashed for the exit.

He brushed the grime from his jeans as he made his way out. When he passed through, Everett rode up with Rusty in tow. Everett wore the same strained expression Tyler felt, but Tyler motioned to the scoreboard, waiting for his time. When it came a few seconds later, Tyler shook his head.

"Five-point-six. I've done better."

"What happened? Everett asked. "It was as if you lost focus."

Tyler shrugged. "Something shifted in the gear. I don't know what it was. I almost missed the steer, but all the practice runs paid off. I'm swapping out the saddles for the next run."

"Yeah, don't scare me like that." Everett winked at Tyler. "I thought I'd lost my percentage during that run."

Tyler started to flip off the man but had a sensation of being watched. When he glanced around, he realized Kenny had continued to follow them. He waved at the young man, and in an instant, Kenny panicked and sprinted into the crowd where he disappeared.

"You have a new fan," said Everett, who lifting an eyebrow comically.

By the time he'd twisted his lips until he looked like a toothless hermit, he had Tyler chuckling. "Yeah, I could tell from how fast he ran away when I waved at him."

Everett shrugged and checked his watch. "Let's get the saddle changed and ready for the next round."

Chapter Three

Tyler sat on the edge of the dance floor, nursing his first drink of the evening. To be honest, it had been warm and half-full for the last hour, but he'd learned years ago that unless he wanted to get plastered, he needed to keep a bottle close. Everyone liked to buy the winner a beer — or worse, a shot of whiskey. His strategy was working tonight.

He might not have wanted to be drunk but Tyler would have welcomed company. He wouldn't have minded finding someone for the evening, but Tyler didn't see how his night could include anything intimate. The closest gay club would be in Norman, but he wasn't interested in a place filled with glitter-smeared twinks. Besides, he wasn't in high demand. At two-hundred fifty pounds, he didn't have the body type to draw any of the typical crowd, not even for a one-night stand. So, he chatted with the well-wishers and watched the room full of straight couples dance themselves into delirium.

"You just going to sit here and hope they come to you? I'm not sure you'll have much luck with the poor steer wrestler routine."

Tyler motioned Everett to a chair beside him. "Have a seat. I'll buy you a beer. You can keep me company before you go searching for one to cut from the herd."

Tyler signaled for another drink, and when Everett settled into his chair, Tyler brought up the equipment malfunction he'd had during his first round. "I checked the saddle. I couldn't see a single reason for what happened."

Everett shrugged, took a drink and studied the crowd. "We'll want to be sure everything is okay before each go. If we're going for National Finals, we can't have technical crap causing you to lose seconds."

Tyler nodded in agreement but saw Lee coming toward him with a guy who looked like a nervous wreck. He also seemed familiar. His appearance was one Tyler found hot as hell. *Another attractive straight guy. Damn, I'd love to run my hands over the sexy, dark beard covering his face.* Tyler scolded himself for drooling over the stud. He'd been down that path before and it hadn't ended well. Before he could dwell on his past bad choices, Lee and the cute dude arrived at the table where he and Everett sat.

"Evening, Tyler. Micah and I were talking about your runs today and what a great bulldogger you are. Then I spotted you over here and thought I'd introduce the two of you."

Tyler caught the subtle hint from the innocent statement but he wasn't certain what he should do about it, other than not to act like a backwoods hick. He stuck his hand out and gave Micah his warmest greeting.

"Nice to meet you, Micah. I'm Tyler Lang, but I guess you already know."

He smiled at the firm grip of Micah's returned handshake. But there was a slight tremor in his voice when Micah spoke. "Good to meet you, too. I'm Micah Vella. Our ranch borders yours on the south side."

Tyler released Micah and studied the rancher. "I knew I recognized you from somewhere else. You were a few grades ahead of me in school."

Micah's face turned crimson. "That's me. I kind of kept to myself during those years. It's flattering that you remembered me. I'm not the most memorable guy."

Tyler studied Micah for a short time before saying, "I won't have any trouble remembering you."

Lee chuckled while Everett lifted an eyebrow at the pair. Their response shook Tyler, and his stomach knotted when he realized what he had done. He started to apologize for his comment to Micah but Lee spoke first.

"Hey, Everett, I bought a hand-braided headpiece today. It's in the truck. Interested in getting a peek at it?"

Everett was halfway out of his chair before he answered. "Sure! I'd love to see it." A second later, Tyler and Micah were alone at the table, and Tyler still had an apology to deliver.

"Sorry about the comment. I didn't intend to make you uncomfortable. I have shit for brains when I'm around sexy guys." He lowered his voice so only Micah could hear him. "Also, I'm gay, and you're hot. Hopefully, that doesn't freak you out. Sometimes, whatever pops into my head comes out of my mouth."

To Tyler's surprise, Micah seemed more embarrassed than angry, since he turned bright red. Tyler watched, uncertain what to do as Micah struggled to speak. He wondered if Micah was another homophobic straight guy, freaking out that a dude had given him a compliment. After a few more seconds had passed, he reached his limits and started to leave so Micah could deal with his issues. But as he pushed the chair back, Micah leaned close and whispered.

"Me, too."

It took Tyler a moment before the two words clicked into his brain. He could kick himself for being so dense. But he needed to be certain he'd understood right. With their gazes locked he asked, "You're gay, too?"

Micah looked about to explode but nodded in agreement. A few seconds passed before he stammered, "Y-Yeah, I'm gay. You're damn hot. It's cool you think I'm decent-looking, too."

Tyler grew a smile, his expression probably as all-encompassing as Micah's. He leaned closer and made a proposal. "Mom bought me a new combo rig that's half horse trailer and half living quarters. It's amazing. I've never seen one like it. It was my graduation present for her son, the steer wrestler."

"Sounds great. Very unique."

Tyler's grin never lessened as he winked at Micah. "You want to see it?"

Micah said, "That would be fun as hell."

Tyler motioned for him to follow. They exchanged a quick glance as they made their way to their pickups. Tyler constantly looked back to make certain Micah hadn't turned to go somewhere else. Each time he saw Micah's deep blue truck behind him, his heart thumped faster. A few minutes later, they pulled into the winding main driveway of the Lang ranch.

Tyler parked beside Micah and looked amazed as the rancher stared in astonishment at the new rig. The matched setup had to be any cowboy's fantasy, at least for machinery. Daydreams about people would be a whole different story. The trailer and truck displayed *Tyler Lang — World Champion Collegian Steer Wrestling*. There was an abundance of room for his horse, along with tons of storage and living quarters larger than many student apartments.

"For the record, I didn't ask for this monstrosity. I spent three days in our largest pasture figuring out how to drive with it before taking it on the road. I'm a passable driver now but still learning."

Micah spread his arms, overwhelmed by the sight before him. "It's huge — and beautiful. That'll make quite an impact on your competitors. It's got to be intimidating for other people."

"Yeah, that's what Mom said, too. She's big on playing with people's minds but I guess that's why she's such a successful Realtor."

"Well, it's an impressive rig."

Tyler's smile broadened. "Want to see inside?"

An odd expression flashed across Micah's face but he nodded. "Absolutely! I'd love the tour."

Tyler opened the door and motioned him into the living area. Micah climbed the steps and paused with his mouth gaping open. "Good Lord, this is bigger and nicer than the places I lived before coming home to take care of the ranch. The layout covers everything possible, down to the huge bed you've got over the fifth wheel."

With a flourish of his hand, Tyler continued. "So, this would be the living room, dining room, kitchen and rec room portion of the tour. Behind that door is the toilet and shower." He motioned toward the almost-invisible hatch at the back of the tiny space. "And last but not least, a secret exit to where the horse stays." Tyler studied the space and frowned. "It sounded so much more impressive before I said it."

Micah laughed and shook his head. "It's amazing. I've never been in anything like it. You did fine."

Tyler flicked a quick glanced to the bed but said nothing. Instead, he relaxed in the role of host. "I've got beer in the fridge. How does that sound? They're from a microbrewery down south. They make damn good beer."

Micah hesitated, but as Tyler started to be concerned, he plunged into the conversation. "Sure, a drink would be great, and good hand-crafted brews are fantastic."

He opened what was disguised as a cabinet door to expose a small refrigerator. Tyler fished out two bottles and held them up so Micah could choose. He accepted the dark brew from Tyler and popped open the lid while Tyler pulled off his boots and eased into a chair. He motioned at the other one. "Have a seat. This place is supposed to be lived in, not looked at."

Micah slid into the offered chair, settling in beside Tyler, but continued to study the room. Tyler nodded and took another drink of his beer. He swirled his bottle and stared at Micah for a minute before smiling.

"We have Lee to blame for this. He's always playing matchmaker for me, even though I've asked him not to do it," Micah said.

"Well, the gesture wasn't wasted. I got to see you," Tyler said with a smile he'd used several times before as an effective lure. It clearly must have had an impact on Micah, whose face turned red as he squirmed, but then the reality of the situation settled itself back into place as Micah spoke.

"That's sweet, but I'm sure you can do better than a brunet who's a foot shorter than you — and only out to one person." Micah rolled his eyes and tilted his head.

"Well, I guess now there are two people who know." He cocked a brow.

Tyler considered him for a moment before taking another drink. Still keeping his silence, he got each of them a second beer and sank into his chair before speaking again. "First, I love guys who are shorter and muscular. I don't get why. And dark hair is so fucking hot. I could run my fingers through it all day. My biggest question is…how close does the carpet match the drapes?"

Micah chuckled and appeared to relax. "It's a close match. No worries there."

Tyler turned more serious as he studied Micah. "When you come out—and to whom—is your business. Even though I'm glad he did, Lee shouldn't have tried to out you. That should have been your choice, not his. I won't tell anyone."

They sat in the quiet for a few seconds before Tyler added. "But I would like to get to know you better." He grinned at Micah. "I'm not talking about any horizontal mambo, either—just spending time, getting more familiar with each other." There was a pop in the distance, and when they looked out the window, they saw a cascade of white streaks trailing over the northern sky. They'd just faded when two additional explosions yielded similar blooms of fire, this time in tones of blue. Tyler turned to Micah and said, "I'd forgotten about the display tonight. We can get a decent viewing from here. How do you feel about watching the display with me? I'm a huge geek about fireworks."

"I love them, too," Micah said. "That would be great to watch them and not deal with the traffic afterward."

Tyler glanced around and settled his gaze back on Micah with his mouth twisted in concern. "I don't have any deck chairs and we could see it a lot better from there."

Micah glanced around. "How opposed are you to looking country?"

Tyler snickered. "I don't give a shit. Besides, who'd know? We're in the middle of nowhere. What're you thinking?"

"That we carry the couch outside and enjoy the show from there."

Another trio of pyrotechnics lit up the sky and Tyler decided. "Great idea! We need to hurry."

In the matter of a few minutes, the couch was positioned for maximum viewing. Tyler glanced around then grabbed a table from the living room.

Micah gave him a questioning expression.

"For drinks — and goodies."

"Snacks?"

Tyler answered as a volley of screamers erupted with an earsplitting whistle. "Yes, the snacks I'll be making now that we have the seating worked out."

He disappeared into the trailer and soon had a bag of popcorn cooking in the microwave while he gathered a few munchies from the fridge. Tyler's secret passion was good cheese, and he had a mixed tray he'd picked up for himself at a favorite shop in Norman.

"You better hurry," Micah called. "There are good ones going off now."

"I'm almost there. Grab us another beer and it'll be ready."

Micah appeared at the door, pulled out two more of the craft beers and motioned toward Tyler. "We're going to drain your stock unless champion bulldoggers winnings are a lot more than I think."

Tyler laughed as he poured the hot popcorn into a bowl and grabbed it, along with the cheese platter.

Micah stayed right on his heels with a brew for each of them. Another volley of fireworks exploded across the horizon as they got comfortable. By the time the finale lit up the northern sky, the beer and food were exhausted. But in the process of watching the exhibition, Micah had cuddled against Tyler. Tyler had reciprocated and draped his arm over Micah's shoulder. As the final flickers of light faded from the sky, darkness crept near. Soon the sounds of night surrounded them.

Micah pulled away and slapped his arm. Then he screwed up his face. "Sorry…mosquito."

Tyler untangled them from each other then stood. "I guess we should take this inside. I'm not a big fan of feeding the wildlife."

Micah nodded and gathered the bottles and plates that had found their way outside during the massive display. It didn't take long before they wrestled the couch back in place and finished taking care of the other debris from their celebration. Tyler dropped the last of the bottles into the recycling bin and turned to find Micah standing, appearing lost.

Tyler thought his expression was adorable. They settled onto the leather sofa, moved closer and shared soft caresses until Tyler could feel the shallow gasps of Micah's breath against the palm of his hand. Tyler caressed the dark scruff etched across Micah's face. The texture running under his touch sent waves of pleasure from his fingertips to spread through his body. "I love your beard. It feels so good." Tyler sighed as he kept up his intimate petting. "I can't grow one for shit. It's like those want-to-be mustaches that fifteen-year-olds sport."

Micah's laugh sounded a little strained, but Tyler found himself drawn more to the man with each passing moment. Then he faltered in his play for Micah. Somehow, this seemed to be something he didn't want to mess up. Each touch became more awkward until Tyler tensed. After a few seconds, he went for broke and moved so his lips touched Micah's ear in a fleeting kiss. A swirl of heady scents filled Tyler and left him lightheaded. *That's what a real cowboy smells like.*

Micah hesitated but cupped Tyler's face between his palms. "What happened to just getting acquainted?"

Tyler's heart dropped as he thought about Micah's apparent lack of enthusiasm. *I always push too hard and end up alone. Damn it. I hope I haven't caused a train wreck.* But then he realized Micah had made no move to end the evening. After a pause, Tyler tried again with a dialed-down version of himself.

"Sure, getting to know each other would be good. I guess we haven't kept up since you graduated from high school — and I finished college," Tyler said. "What would you like to ask?"

Micah cocked his head and studied Tyler before speaking again. "Why do you like bulldogging? I mean…now you're a champion and stuff, but how did you get there?"

Tyler chuckled and relaxed against the sofa. "I drove Mom crazy. I had to be entertained all the time. As I got older, she let me go places with my uncle and older cousin. My uncle ran a small rodeo and my cousin rode bulls. I shadowed him and wanted to do everything he did." He gave Micah a significant expression. "That didn't work with my mother. She refused to let her son ride a crazy bull."

"You never tried?"

Tyler winked at Micah and chuckled. "Now, I never said that. I bugged my uncle until he let me ride a good-sized calf."

Micah cocked an eyebrow. "I'm guessing that didn't go well."

Tyler puckered his lips and shook his head. "I lasted until the first buck. After that, I had a mouth full of dirt and an impressive collection of bruises. Mom found out and had a fit. She forbade Uncle Steve from letting me ever ride another bull."

Micah chuckled and wagged his finger at Tyler. "So being the good son, you never climbed on another one. But your promise kept you off the bulls and onto the steers."

"You've got it. I did what she'd asked of me."

Micah studied him. "And when did she find out about the steer wrestling? She couldn't have been happy about it."

Tyler considered the question before answering. "The summer I turned fourteen, before starting my freshman year in high school."

"How did it go?"

Tyler dug through the memories of those days and grew a grin. "Talk about a rough year. Mom's world got shook. That summer, I told her I was gay."

The expression on Micah's face became somber. "How did that go? She seems fine with it now."

"It never got bad, nothing like other people have dealt with. She finished several glasses of mint julep before she came back to talk about it. By then, I had no intention of being something other than myself, so it didn't take much for the two of us to agree. But we never disagreed about who I intended to be. At that point, she realized I would do whatever I wanted and she couldn't change me. Then she made a smart decision." Tyler grinned from ear to ear, and after they had sat in silence for a brief time, Micah asked what Tyler had left hanging.

"Okay, what's the smart thing she did?"

"She supports me in whatever I want to do. Some of my weird ideas ended up taking care of themselves, so I narrowed it down to two things for her. First, dudes turned me on."

Micah said, "And what was number two?"

"That I got a rush from jumping off my horse and throwing a steer onto the ground."

Micah studied Tyler for a moment but a huge yawn developed.

"It's late and all the drunk idiots will be out after trying to blow up stuff. Why don't we clean up and you can spend the night?"

Micah cocked an eyebrow. "On the couch?"

Tyler gave him a charming smile. "I think that would be part of the whole 'getting to know each other before we jump each other's bones' thing."

Micah leaned in and gave Tyler a quick peck on the cheek. "I think we're moving a lot closer to the 'jumping each other' part."

Tyler's grin got wider. "So, there's still hope?"

"Oh, yeah. There's lots of hope. I'm counting on you chasing after me."

"But tonight…" Tyler cut his eyes to the couch.

Micah lifted an eyebrow before he burst into a wide smile again. "Yes, for now, it's going to be separate sleeping accommodations."

Chapter Four

Micah wasn't moving too fast. The sun was intense, even with the shade of his hat and wearing the darkest sunglasses he owned. *How many of those craft beers did I drink last night? I had no idea they packed such a punch.*

He walked one of the horses into the exercise pen before grabbing a wheelbarrow and shovel to clean the stall. The smell of the cedar chips they used for bedding didn't make his stomach tie itself in knots, unlike everything he'd considered for breakfast. Eventually, he settled for a sport drink he'd grabbed at the convenience store on his way home.

"Rough night, son?"

Micah tensed but didn't turn back to his dad until he'd released the mare. He watched her gallop around the pen a few times with her tail arched behind her. He'd hoped his father would have left him to recover in silence but there was no surprise when he hadn't moved an inch and seemed to enjoy Micah's squirming. He sighed and turned to deal with the situation.

"Watching fireworks with a friend. A few good beers that had me uncomfortable driving home after." He studied his father. *Something's wrong. His color is off, too.* "Dad, you hate doctors. I get that. But I'd like to have someone take a look at you. I'll make you an appointment with Dr. Patel."

"You'll have to set it up with my social secretary. I don't think I have an opening until next spring. We might be able to pencil you in sometime in April. How would that work for you?" his father replied.

"Yeah, I'll schedule it between your weekly domino nights. Why don't you get some rest?"

"I'll have plenty of time to do nothing but rest soon enough. I'll feed the chickens, check on that damn bull and see if we have any new baby calves this morning. When you're finished, come in the house and I'll make you some sunny-side-up eggs."

Micah swallowed hard to keep from puking. "I'm good with breakfast. I need to check with Lee and find out when we can set a time to work on that section of fence. It shouldn't take me long, if you think you'll be okay."

He earned an arched eyebrow. "I'll have you know, young man, that I've wiped your butt. I'm capable of taking care of a few chores while you're chatting with Lee."

An expression of happiness grew across his dad's face and Micah knew it was time to give up that argument.

But as his father ambled down the path to the corral, he continued the discussion. "Dad, I'll make you an appointment with the doctor. You keep saying it's just old age, but I'd like for you to see someone, and if they need to do tests, we can take care of them."

His dad paused and studied him for quite some time before shrugging. "If it'll make you happy, go ahead. It won't change a damn thing."

Micah knew he'd hit a nerve with his dad for him to have cursed. For most people, it wouldn't have even warranted a blink. With George Vella, saying 'damn' was no casual slip. Micah kept his concerns to himself as the man who'd raised him resumed his journey to care for the horses.

Once his father had disappeared from view, Micah picked up his pace. In less than an hour he was on his way to the Lang ranch to talk with Lee. As he drove through the enormous brick-and-iron gate, he felt intimidated. Even the house Lee had as farm manager had more square footage than Micah's home.

Tyler's mother shot past him in a vehicle that seemed to be worth more than the Vella's entire ranch. She had a phone pressed against one ear and her attention wasn't on driving as she swerved to avoid crashing into Micah's truck. *Like Dad always said, money don't buy happiness. I wonder if that isn't true for Tyler's mother.*

He spotted Lee at one of the barns that dotted the ranch and Micah headed toward him. As he got closer, he realized Lee wasn't alone. Tyler stood beside Lee while an unfamiliar kid stood a few steps behind the others — and didn't seem happy in any way, shape or form. Micah coasted his truck to a stop beside Lee's and watched the trio. After the past night, his feelings about Tyler weren't clear. As he considered the fallout if he ran like a quail to home, Tyler saw him, waved and flashed him that thousand-watt grin. *Dammit. Now I'm screwed.*

Lee turned to him, and Micah almost groaned. Micah read the smirk on his face. He figured Lee had seen him around first light when he'd slipped out of Tyler's trailer and driven home. It wasn't like Micah had gotten lucky the previous night. Well, not in the big sense of the word. He might try to explain the details, but it wouldn't be any better. After a second or two, Micah decided the kid was happier than him. *Suck it up, Micah. It's your own damn fault.*

He climbed out of the truck and moved to meet them halfway. He exchanged a handshake with Lee, then Tyler. The kid had trailed behind them and looked shocked when Micah extended his hand.

"Micah Vella. My family owns the ranch just north of here."

The teenager took his hand in a decent grip, but even listening closely, Micah couldn't understand what he'd said. He shook his head. "Sorry... Didn't quite catch that."

This time he tensed and glanced at Tyler before speaking again. "Sorry. I'm Kenny. Kenny Evans."

Micah pumped his hand again and shot him a smile. "Nice to meet you, Kenny."

Kenny nodded and slipped back into the shade cast by the barn. After the silence stretched out too long, Micah decided that whatever the reason for Kenny to be here, the kid wasn't happy. But when he turned back to Lee and Tyler, he wanted to hide, too. He needed to get things rolling, regardless of how uncomfortable these two made him.

"Hey, guys. We need to talk about replacing the barbed wire fence. I hoped there might be a time when Lee could help. You've been changing out your old fences and I thought I'd see if you wanted to split the cost."

As soon as the last word left Micah's lips, Tyler jumped onto the discussion. "That'd be great. I hate the old wire. We've had a couple horses get nasty cuts from it. Besides, Mom would like to replace all the existing fence with the polymer-rail stuff we've used in all the new paddocks."

Dollar signs spun through Micah's head at the cost of Tyler's fence. What they were using was absolutely top-of-the-line and probably more expensive than the combined miles of fence on his entire ranch. He gathered his thoughts to explain the problem to Tyler but realized he hadn't finished presenting his idea.

Tyler was saying, "That stuff costs a fortune, and we're the ones that need the new fencing for the horses." He stopped and seemed to do some mental calculations. An instant later, Tyler smiled back at him. "What if you help with the labor, and maybe some maintenance, and we'll pay for materials? Will that work for you?"

Micah's mouth dropped open as he stared at Tyler. While he recovered from the shock, he considered his options. Part of him was yelling to take the offer and not question Tyler's assessment but the rest of him that wanted life to be fair was having a screaming fit that was impossible to ignore. He took a deep breath, let it ease out and explained. "I agree about not splitting it in half, but it's not fair for you to pay for everything. What if we cover the cost as if it were a regular barbed wire fence then you pay the rest?"

Tyler didn't miss a beat. He grabbed Micah's hand in a tight handshake then drew them together and thumped on his back. The bro hug lasted a little longer than it typically might, and when Micah glanced at Lee, his friend arched his eyebrows.

Tyler seemed to try to ignore Lee while the heat of embarrassment flashed across his face. Before he could respond, Tyler turned to Kenny, who had faded into the background. "Helping build fence will be good for you, and we can finish it in a few days. What do you think of that idea?"

Kenny's gaze darted to each man before settling on Tyler. "Sounds fine," he said.

Micah turned his focus back to Tyler before continuing. "We can start as soon as you get the materials. How long do you think it will take?"

Lee considered the question for a moment then answered Micah. "The company we bought the fencing from likes us a lot. I bet they'll get it to us early next week."

Micah started to confirm, but Tyler spoke first. "I have a rodeo this weekend but I'll be back in time to help."

The idea of working with Tyler left Micah with a tremble in his stomach. But when he checked his watch, his focus changed in an instant. "Shit! I gotta go. I'm already running behind."

Tyler regarded him with an expression of concern. "Anything we can help with?"

Micah chuckled. "Not unless you want to take my dad to the doctor. And yes, if you think that's the last place he wants to go, you would be right." With a sprinkling of laughs and chuckles, the group broke apart. Even Kenny seemed happy.

But the scene Micah found himself in a few hours later had no sign of even a fragment of humor. From the argument to get his dad into the truck to the hour-long wait for an exam room to sitting in the tiny space with George perched on the table as miserable as Micah could remember, this had the makings of a day he'd like to never repeat. After a few minutes of painful silence, Micah sighed. "You're pissed off, but we need to check on what's wrong. Hopefully it'll be nothing and I can leave you with your cache of Pepsi. So, humor me."

George puckered up like he'd drunk a shot of pickle juice. "It's a waste of money. They're just going to say it's old age and send me home."

"I'll be happy to take you to the house, fix you a huge bowl of ice cream and let you watch all the episodes of *Jeopardy* you'd like."

He shifted on the table before catching Micah's eye. "I'm holding you to that promise." He was about to add more when there was a light knock at the door and the doctor came into the room. Micah didn't know much about him, other than he'd heard he was blunt as hell and the best internist in the state. Micah was willing to tolerate a rough bedside manner if the man's skills were as good as he'd heard.

The doctor set down the notebook computer all medical professionals seemed to be attached to these days and studied the screen. He went through the questions in rapid-fire succession until Micah's frustration built. But when he glanced at his dad, George just smirked.

Once the barrage of questions ended, the doctor began the physical part of the examination. When he checked George's eyes, there was a change in the doctor's demeanor. What a few seconds before had felt cursory now appeared to become more thorough and methodical. Time slowed to a crawl and Micah's anxiety ratcheted higher with each passing second.

After what seemed an eternity, the doctor stepped back and locked gazes with George.

"I'm sending you to Oklahoma City for tests. The nurse will work with you to set them up for either today or tomorrow, but I want them done right away."

Micah swallowed the bile that had filled his mouth and fought to keep from choking. "What tests?"

He typed away at his keyboard and didn't look up as he replied. "A CT scan, perhaps a needle biopsy. Depends on what they find."

George said, "We're busy today. We might be able to work it in later next week."

The doctor scowled and pursed his lips. "You're jaundiced and have lost weight, neither of which are good signs. I would suggest you follow my recommendation."

"Dad," Micah said, "we're going to Oklahoma City."

* * * *

Tyler stood outside in only a pair of lounge pants and yawned as the dawn crept up the horizon. Seeing the rancher the previous week had done nothing but increase his attraction. Last weekend, there had been another rodeo on his long list, and he relished the resulting win, even days later. He walked to the edge of the deck he'd built to match his trailer, lifted the enormous mug of coffee to his lips and enjoyed a healthy drink. A loud whinny from Rusty punctuated Tyler's enjoyment of the morning. He'd given his horse the equine equivalent of a spa day and released him into one of the lush paddocks close to the house. The horse was taking advantage of the opportunity to graze himself into oblivion.

Tyler drank the last of his coffee, slipped his hand down his pants and scratched himself. At that point, he almost launched into the dawn sky at the sound of Lee's voice.

"How's your morning?"

He grinned at the cowboy who'd somehow sneaked up beside him, leading one of their brood mares. He pulled his hand out of his pants and smirked at Lee. "I guess I'll spare you the handshake. What are you doing up so early?"

"Micah's meeting me where he's replacing the old fencing. Looks like the poor roping calves will lose their prime eats now that we can put horses in that pasture."

Tyler nodded as if he agreed, but his mind rested more on the hot rancher who'd be working with Lee. He attempted to keep the lecherous smirk from creeping onto his face. From the chuckle coming from Lee, he'd been an epic fail. Tyler wondered what was going on when opinionated Lee shifted his focus and seemed to be willing to let his gaze settled on anyone but Tyler.

When it continued for a good while, Tyler cocked his brows. "What's up? You look like a kid caught stealing watermelons."

Lee rolled his eyes but a grin grew back on his face. "I was just wondering if you wanted to help with the fencing."

A smile slipped across his mouth at the idea of working with Micah, but he refused to be too easy a target for Lee. "I'm not sure. Maybe. I've got a long to-do list I need to take care of before I'm gone to the next rodeo."

"That's true. There's always the next rodeo. I'll be heading out to meet Micah in a few minutes, if you want a break." Lee continued to wherever he was taking the mare but then stopped again. "The kid's here, too. I have him cleaning stalls, but I thought I'd take him with us to work on the fence."

Tyler nodded sagely but saw his opportunity. "Oh, yeah, Kenny. I forgot about him. Well, that settles it. I have to go, since he was my idea. I better get dressed. I'll meet you at the barn and help you load everything."

Lee continued past him but Tyler had no difficulty seeing the expression of devilry plastered over his face. Tyler refused to rise to the bait, turning to make his way across the deck and into the sleeping quarters. He scanned the room for a minute and beamed.

Some people thought it was odd he didn't stay at the ranch house his mother had built, but those rooms had never felt like his. This space was a tenth the size of his bedroom, but it was all his. It had the aesthetic of a twenty-something guy, too. *This is what I am. Everything in here I picked out, and I paid for.* He'd selected the rig, too, but his mother had insisted on getting it for him as a graduation present. He'd argued until he'd found out that what he'd wanted cost more than most houses in this part of the country. So, he'd let her win the argument and hoped that with his winnings, the rig would be the last thing she had to buy for him.

He shook off the woolgathering and stripped. As he went through his clothing, he scratched his stomach while he considered his options. It didn't take long to grab a pair of Wranglers with holes in strategic spots and a T-shirt that showed off his muscular chest. He considered underwear but decided it would ruin the effect from the slash the jeans featured across his ass. It didn't show much, but it created some eye candy.

Satisfied with everything else, he tugged on his work boots and made a dash for the door. He arrived at the pickup in time to help Lee and Kenny load the fencing they wanted to complete that day. It would be the entire section of fence, that was certain. They climbed into the manual-gear pickup and it clearly didn't take Kenny long to realize that dodging the gear shift was something he needed to do well for his own self-preservation. It didn't help for Lee to choose the roughest possible path to where he planned to meet Micah.

They drew up to an ancient corner-post, jumped out and headed to the fence to greet Micah. Tyler squeezed his hand in a long shake then winked. The combination had the effect he was shooting for. Micah's face turned scarlet and his eyes grew in size. About the time Micah started squirming, Lee assigned tasks. Tyler knew whose side the ranch manager was on as he tried to help Micah reach a level of calm. But Tyler had every intention of enjoying himself.

"Okay," Lee said, "let's get this stuff laid out so we can take down the old fence." His gaze darted toward the kid. "Kenny, you'll need a pair of heavy leather gloves or your hands will be torn up. In the tool box behind the seat of the pickup, there should be some extras."

Kenny nodded and raced to the truck. He reappeared a minute later, tugging on the gloves. Tyler felt responsible for Kenny. He didn't want the kid hurt. That hadn't been his point when he'd suggested the kid work at the farm. He grabbed a couple of pair of fencing pliers and motioned for Kenny to follow. He used the hook end of the tool to remove the aged staples from the fence, showing Kenny the technique that would work best. Tyler watched for a brief time before stepping in to help. "You don't need to beat them to death, just get them out. Here…try this."

Tyler chose a hammer from the pickup and showed Kenny how to use the two tools together to pry the metal loops from the ancient wood. After a couple of adjustments in technique, Kenny could take out fence staples with a minimum of drama and only a few muttered profanities. He waited for a minute to be certain Kenny understood what he was doing then rejoined Lee and Micah where they were rolling the old barbed wire into coils that would be easy to deal with. He donned a pair of leather gloves as he moved beside Micah. When the rancher looked up, Tyler flashed what he hoped was his warmest smile.

"Morning, Micah," Tyler said as he held out his gloved hand. Micah took the offered greeting with only slight trepidation. With a mischievous chuckle, Tyler pulled Micah into a tight bro hug. He heard a gasp escape but didn't relent.

Lee stopped, leaned against the shovel he had been holding and chuckled. "You two need some privacy?"

Tyler considered taking it up a level and planting a kiss on Micah's oh-so-hot lips, but a quick glance confirmed that Kenny had slowed and was waiting to see what they did. The result seemed to have Micah squirming like a newborn chick trying to escape its shell. Tyler enjoyed clowning around, but he didn't want to ruin what he would like to think was a developing relationship.

He released Micah with a huge thump on the back. He turned to Lee and winked. "Nope, I don't need it private. I'm doing fine right here."

Lee turned back to pulling posts with a chuckle and a shake of his head while Micah and Kenny looked anywhere but at either of them while they kept busy. With a look of satisfaction, Tyler set to work taking down the old wire.

The fiery summer day beat down with the ferocity typical for the season. The hot, dry wind had all the refreshment of a blast furnace. An hour or so later found all of them stripped from the waist up, having left their sweat-drenched shirts thrown onto the pickup to dry. Tyler tolerated the pounding heat but found himself having difficulty not staring at Micah, enjoying the rancher's pale skin with its dusting of hair. The sweat running down Micah's chest made him even more attractive for Tyler and he had about as much control over it as a moth at a bug zapper. But he had no intention of being fried. He considered himself more the zapper than the zapped. After he recalled their night together, Tyler realized his cock had swelled until it created an obvious bulge in his jeans.

"I got to take a leak. Be right back," Micah said, giving Tyler the chance he had been waiting for.

"Me, too. It's time to drain—" He glanced at Kenny. "I need to pee, too. There's a spot over here that's kind of private."

The two headed toward the thicket of cedars that dominated a small gully. As they threaded their way through the branches, Tyler overheard a discussion between Lee and Kenny. *Seems Lee doesn't like the idea of the kid following us. Not that I would pull anything, but I don't mind that Lee took care of one cock-blocker — two, if I count Lee himself.*

But with Kenny left behind, it would give him the time to work on his connection with Micah. In a few steps, they would reach the spot he had in mind and hoped it would work to bring them closer. But as they stopped, Micah seemed disinterested in anything other than emptying his bladder. Tyler went for the big prize and stepped beside his quarry. He took a few seconds to fish out his plumped cock. He glanced in Micah's direction, caught the cowboy taking a peek and Tyler gave him a small smile.

As he finished, Micah shook his cock a few times, which only made Tyler's dick regain its former hardness. Any moisture in Tyler's mouth left with the dry Oklahoma wind and he found himself reduced to the awkwardness of a pubescent junior-high kid. As he considered the sight beside him, he felt more awkward than he had in years. He moved closer, but after being turned down the last time he'd made a play, he wasn't as confident about putting moves on Micah.

A few seconds later he passed the desire to keep anything in check—especially himself. He fell into Micah's deep brown eyes. Tyler ran his tongue over his parched lips. He closed the distance between then and cupped Micah's face between his meaty hands and pulled him close. Their lips had barely touched when Tyler whispered, "You're fucking hot. You up for a little fun?"

Micah's Adam's apple bobbed up and down for a few seconds before he nodded. Tyler reacted with the pent-up passion he already had for the rancher. Holding Micah tightly, he hungrily unleashed his lust by crushing their lips together. Tyler probed Micah's mouth. A few seconds later, they pulled apart, both gasping for breath.

"We don't have long. You okay with this?"

In a whisper almost lost to the wind, Micah replied, "Yes. I want it."

Without another word, he reached between Micah's legs and wrapped his fingers around the now-stiff cock. He squeezed tight and enjoyed the moan that sounded. Tyler focused on their moment of intimacy as he stroked Micah while he leaned in and gnawed down the side of his neck.

The sounds of pleasure ran from Micah's lips as Tyler allowed himself a moment to enjoy the sight of Micah's dick while he worked his way up and down the shaft with his thick fist.

Micah grabbed his face and pulled Tyler in for another kiss. Surprised at first, Tyler returned the attention, finding the sensation of Micah's stubble against his lips amazing. He bit, nipped and stroked his way across Micah as the rancher struggled to fuck Tyler's hand. Micah let out a few short gasps before the first white strand shot across the ground. Tyler enjoyed the sight as thick lines of white decorated the earth in front of them. Micah shuddered as Tyler milked out the last of the hot semen.

The instant the last drop of cum hit the ground, Micah pawed at Tyler's jeans, trying to free his cock from the form-fitted material. It only took seconds for Tyler's dick to be encased in Micah's steel grip. He pinched and tugged Tyler's nipples while he stroked his cock. The combination of sensations sent Tyler's head spinning. His pleasure only grew when Micah nipped on his neck. He relaxed against the muscular rancher and let the sensations surround him. It took no longer than a minute before Tyler enjoyed the familiar waves of ecstasy signaling the beginning of his orgasm.

Then Micah ran his free hand across Tyler's chest and teased his nipple again. He pinched and tugged at them as Tyler's excitement built.

"Yeah, that. Harder," Tyler said.

Micah gave one a hard twist and the sensation sent Tyler crashing over the edge. With Micah pumping him like a wild man, his body contracted and the crest of euphoria sent him to levels he hadn't known with anyone else. He lost himself, relishing the orgasm as he lay in Micah's arms. His first conscious thought focused on the tender kisses Micah planted down his neck. His body shook with each wave of pleasure until a final translucent strand fell to the ground. Micah's sweet touch on his cock and balls left Tyler swimming in the euphoria of their hot act.

The seconds ticked past unheeded until Tyler turned himself in Micah's embrace. He ran his finger over Micah's flushed-red lips and gave him a heartfelt smile. "That was amazing. Beyond mind-blowing."

Tyler slipped his hands over Micah's bare chest when they both froze at a distinct sound. Tyler backed away, tugging on his jeans as fast as possible. In less time than he'd imagined, they were making their way back to the worksite.

As they cleared the trees, Tyler's anxiety increased at the expression Lee wore. But it was Micah who asked, "What's up?"

"You left your phone in the cab and someone's called three or four times. I checked the screen. It was your dad."

Micah expression shifted to one of dire concern as he punched the redial button. The expression on Micah's face put Tyler's stomach in knots. The tension grew as they waited. Then George's voice came through the speaker. "Micah?"

"Hey, Dad, what's up?"

There was a pause as Micah listened with his face becoming grave and his mouth pinched. "Okay, so when's the appointment?"

Micah's emotional state seemed to hover close to full-blown panic.

"I'll be home in a minute." There was another short pause then he cut the call.

He grabbed his shirt and pulled it on as he darted his eyes from one thing to another. Tyler recognized what was happening and stepped in.

"Go. Take care of things at home. We'll do the fence stuff. Don't worry about it."

Micah paused for a split second before exhaling in a gust. "Thanks." He glanced around and still seemed worried about leaving.

Tyler grabbed his shoulder and squeezed. "Get home. We got this."

Chapter Five

This isn't good. Doctors don't make same-day appointments to tell you things are fine. If you're well, the nurse just tells you to set up your next visit for six months from now. Damn it, Dad. I've been after you to see a doctor since forever. But Micah kept his thoughts to himself and didn't want to burden his father.

"You won't cure anything by stewing over it. Wait until the doctor goes over the test results," George said.

He wanted to tell his father how mad he was that George hadn't seen a doctor earlier, but then he would come across as a complete ass and that wouldn't help. With a sigh, he ground his knuckles into his eyes until it felt like he was using a hoof rasp on them. But when he stopped, George still wore the same expression. He threw his hands up in exasperation. "Where is he? He's the one who wanted to see you today."

"He's a busy man. He'll be here soon and explain what they found in all those tests. Take a deep breath and calm down."

"Don't you think—" Micah said, but there was a knock and his attention shifted to the door. He focused on the doctor as he sat his computer on the counter. He studied the screen for a second then turned to George.

He spoke with no interlude. "The results of your tests came back today, and we need to move on this. They confirmed that you have pancreatic cancer. Fortunately, they indicate a neuroendocrine tumor, which has a much better surgical prognosis. My nurse is setting up your surgery for tomorrow at the teaching hospital in Oklahoma City where they will perform a distal pancreatectomy." He stopped and his eyes shifted between the two of them. "This is assuming you want to handle this as aggressively as possible. But the procedure has potential side effects that might be serious and the recovery time can be substantial."

Micah leaned in intently, ready to start. "We want to take care of it and do whatever has the best outcome."

He watched the doctor but soon realized the medical professional was studying George, who was silent. A knot formed in Micah's throat at the thoughtful expression his dad wore.

"Dad?" Micah said.

"Mr. Vella, the decision is yours. The full treatment regimen will be chemotherapy and radiation, along with the surgery. It is something to consider."

Micah's throat tightened until his breath came in tiny gasps. He felt stricken when he met his father's gaze. "Dad, fight it. Surely you want to do whatever you can to survive."

His father studied him for an eternity before he spoke again. When he did, there was an overwhelming sense of sadness in his voice. "Do you remember when your mother was sick? What the treatments did to her?

Toward the end, I think she regretted taking all the poisons into her body. She was miserable. I don't know if I can go through that. Your mother was always so strong and fought to live through the whole ordeal."

Tears welled up in Micah's eyes until he blinked and the trails of sadness ran tracks down his face to drip from his jaw. The thought of losing his dad became unbearable. He knew it was selfish but he wanted his father here, regardless of what it took. He'd lost his mother almost ten years before and still thought about her every day.

Before he cobbled together a response, George reached out and wiped the tears from his face. He gave Micah a well-worn expression. "It's okay to be a little self-centered sometimes." He turned to the doctor and nodded. "What were you saying about the treatments for the best survival rates?"

The rest of their day consisted of setting appointments and being given detailed instructions on what he needed to do to be ready for surgery first thing in the morning. When they reached the ranch later in the afternoon, George moved at a crawl. Micah helped him through the door, fixed him a glass of sweet tea — his dad's favorite — and brought it to him.

"Here, Dad. Get some rest and I'll take care of the animals and your garden."

It indicated how exhausted he was that George didn't argue when Micah volunteered to care for his precious vegetables. Micah turned the television to a well-worn reality outdoor show. He thought this series had something about alligators. He didn't care what the program was, so long as it kept his dad occupied. He located the always-elusive remote and set it within his dad's reach.

"This okay? Is there anything else you need?"

George turned to Micah and pushed him toward the door. "I'm not an invalid. If I'm missing something, I'll call you. That phone of yours is glued to your butt. Go. Don't forget to check for hornworms on the tomatoes. I found a few yesterday." When Micah didn't leave, he waved his hands at his son again. "Get outta here before I get cranky. Someone's coming up the road, anyway."

Micah turned and walked to the doorway then paused. He studied his father as he sat in silhouette against the faint light filtering through the west window. The melancholy of the moment washed over him and he became overwhelmed by the fear of losing George.

"If you don't quit standing there gawking at me, I'm going to plant my boot in your rear."

Micah chuckled through his tears and recalled his dad had said something about visitors. His father was better than the guineas they kept around to let them know when people were coming up the driveway and his dad wasn't as obnoxious about it as the helmet-shaped birds. Right on cue, they announced an arrival. Seconds later, the two dogs rushed to the door and unloaded a barrage of barks. He wasn't too surprised to see Lee's pickup coasting to a stop but shocked would be the more accurate word when Tyler stepped from the passenger side.

They walked around and flanked Micah, their faces etched with concern. Lee seemed to be the one elected to ask the dreaded question. "So, how's your dad?"

Micah spent a moment composing himself and still almost lost it when he finally began speaking. "They found out he has pancreatic cancer but the tests say the tumor hasn't spread, so tomorrow morning they'll take it out." Micah stopped and cleared his throat a few times as he struggled to keep himself together. "Once it's finished, they'll decide what other treatments he needs. The doctor said something about chemo and radiation."

Tyler studied him before speaking. "Sounds like you caught it in time for the surgery to work. That's good news."

Micah wondered why they were visiting when Lee spoke up. "We came over to offer to take care of the animals. That way, you can focus on taking care of your dad."

Micah studied both of them for a while before sighing. "I'd like to think I can take care of everything, but I don't know what his treatment schedule will be like. I guess I should take advantage of any assistance I can get." Micah twisted his lips before frowning. "Yeah, I'd appreciate the help."

A much younger voice sounded from the backseat of Lee's pickup. "I can help, too. Whatever you need."

Micah peered around the vehicle to find Kenny hanging from the window. His volume was more normal. "I'd like to help, too."

"Everyone should relax and not stand around being mopey. We have plenty to do before I have my snip and clip," George said. His silent approach had caught the entire group unaware. But by the time he'd finished lecturing them, they all wore grins. His eyes twinkled as he continued, "None of you know how to take care of my garden the way it needs." He studied each of them then nodded at Kenny.

"Young man, I bet you are smart enough to be a competent gardener. Come with me. We'll get a couple of hoes and weed the garden so you won't need to do as much each day. I'm George, and what's your name?"

"I'm Kenny."

George turned to the others, and Micah saw the twinkle in his eyes. "Kenny and I will weed the garden. That should give the rest of you time to talk about how to wrap everything up. Once y'all finish, you can meet us on the porch for a glass of sweet tea." George walked off without another comment. Kenny stood with his head pivoting between Tyler and George, trying to decide where he should be. He got a nod from Tyler and raced to catch up with George. A soft conversation started between the two. The others waited until they disappeared into a shed before commenting.

"Kenny seems happy to help your dad," Tyler said.

Micah nodded in agreement. "He's a good kid. Kind of quiet. You said he tried to screw up the Independence Day parade?"

"He and a couple of other kids threw fireworks under the horses when we came down the route. Kenny got caught, and he'd planned it, so I ended up with him as a farm hand for the summer." Tyler paused before continuing. "I think it relieved his mother for him to have something to keep him busy so he wouldn't get it more trouble. But I'm glad it wasn't me dealing with her when they got home. She was pissed off."

Micah chuckled as he recalled when he'd gotten a dirty job to help him remember to stay out of trouble. "He isn't the only kid to screw up and clean stalls for a reminder." Micah's insight set them all smiling and nodding.

He saw his dad, armed with a couple of hoes and Kenny on his heels. Their conversation had become more animated and Micah had no difficulty reconstructing the words. He hoped Kenny was more receptive than he'd been at a similar age. He turned back to his friends as the two moved toward George's precious garden. "Let me go through the animals' schedules. I have no intention of letting them finish before we do, because Dad will never let me hear the end of it."

* * * *

Once they'd wrapped up the chores and everyone had left, the night grew to be an all-consuming beast as Micah played scenarios through his mind. He appreciated that Tyler had understood and stayed later. Tyler even offered to stay over to keep Micah company, but he declined the offer. He liked Tyler, to the point he found himself drawn to the young steer wrestler, but they hadn't reached a point where he was comfortable sharing something as serious as his father's illness.

Exhaustion overcame him in the pre-dawn, but shortly afterward, his father's knock echoed from wall to wall in his room. The rap awakened him from a nightmare he'd dredged from some dark part of his mind. He locked away the too-familiar dream as he ducked into the shower and waited for the cold water to wipe the last remnants of sleep from his system. He toweled off and yanked on a change of clothes before stumbling out the front door to find his dad waiting in the pickup.

They spoke little through the hour-long drive. Once they arrived, they were processed with the utmost efficiency. The minutes clicked past and Micah was ready for it all to end.

"Don't forget to check the chickens. We don't want a coyote to get them."

Micah gave his father the expression he reserved for iron-plated dragons, were-unicorns — or his third-grade teacher, Mrs. Stovall, who was both. But he formulated a reply. "You're going in for surgery and all you're worried about is your hens?"

George lifted his eyebrows and shook a finger at Micah. "I've raised all those chickens from chirpers. You can't get real farm-fresh eggs unless you are the one raising them. I put in too much work on them for them to end up as some coyote's dinner."

Some of the tension leaked from Micah when he had no other choice but to laugh at his father. He shook his head as he replied. "You're crazy. You know that, right?"

"Just a happy-go-lucky old fart. That's me."

At that instant, the surgical nurse appeared in the doorway. "Mr. Vella? We're ready to go back." She shifted her focus to Micah. "We'll come get you once he's settled."

Micah nodded and tried to swallow down his fears. George disappeared behind the automatic double door into the 'Staff Only' section. He walked to his chair, fished out his phone and tried to distract himself for what would be a whole series of hurry up and wait sequences. He'd settled in for the first wait when he heard a familiar voice.

"Hey, Micah. How's your dad? We got here as quick as possible. I dumped all of today's work on Lee and his junior helper," Tyler said.

"Hey, Tyler. Mrs. Lang. Thanks for coming, but it's a long surgery. Don't feel like you need to stay the entire time."

"Nope. We're staying—or at least I am. Mom may have to deal with stuff at her office, but I'm here to keep you company." Tyler turned pensive before returning his gaze to Micah. "I dealt with this a few years ago with Mom's breast cancer. It would have been good to have a friend through the mess."

Micah didn't have it in him to argue. If he were being honest, he wanted the company. He didn't want to go through this without a friend to lean on. He would love for it to be more than just him and his dad. After only a brief pause for consideration, he nodded at Tyler and Mary Lou. "I'd welcome some company."

Tyler flopped into the seat next to Micah, spread his arms over the chair backs and looked satisfied. "This'll work fine. We can wait without our butts falling asleep."

Micah chuckled at the comment, but when he got a wink from Tyler, a flash of heat washed over his face. Trying for a distraction, he turned to Mary Lou, only to get another smirk. *Great, both of them are working to embarrass the hell out of me.*

Micah took a moment to regain control before responding. When he did, he targeted Tyler. "I'd appreciate the support. I hope this will turn out well, but I always have a Plan B in the wings." He paused and studied them before continuing. "This time I might have a Plan C, D and E."

Tyler's mom gave him a knowing nod. "With the big C, you're playing it smart to have contingency plans. Sometimes the cure is worse than the disease. Well, it seems so, anyway."

Before the conversation went further, the nurse came to get Micah. He jumped to his feet then realized he needed to deal with Tyler and his mother. At least that was his initial thought, but when he turned to his supporters, they waved him on. "We'll wait here," Tyler said. "I don't think George needs unexpected visitors before he goes into surgery."

Micah nodded then trotted to the person escorting him to his dad. He entered the room to find his father surrounded by bags of fluid and clicking machines. He wasn't sure what to say or do. His dad had always been the one in charge.

"Close your mouth, Micah, before you draw flies."

Out of years of habit, he did as he was told. But a split second later he realized what had happened and turned toward his dad. "You know... One of these days I'll learn not to jump at what you say."

George chuckled at his son. "Nope. It's the work of a lifetime. It won't ever wear off." He lifted his hand where the IV connected him to all the worrisome tubing and a big bag of what looked like water but Micah was certain wasn't. "The leachers have been in, sucking me dry. They stole my clothes, too, but they said they'd give them back when I leave. I told the girl who took them that it was my Sunday-go-to-meeting outfit. She said that in the whole time she's worked here, they've never sent someone home in a hospital gown."

Micah stared at him before shaking his head. "They're going to put you on whatever floor is the funny farm."

His dad patted his hand where he was white-knuckling the rail. "I've been in worse places. You'll end up with an ulcer if you don't learn to relax. Maybe you should find some place where they teach yoga."

The traffic of hospital workers increased before he could respond to the crack, so Micah only had the chance to listen to the questions they peppered his dad with. The room drained of people, and he and George stared at each other. But before he gathered his wits to have any kind of meaningful conversation, another person appeared. "Mr. Vella, I'm Steven and I'll take you down to where they will do your surgery."

Micah leaned in to give his dad a quick peck on the cheek and George patted the side of his face. "It's going to take hours. Go get a burger or something."

Micah rolled his eyes. "I'm not leaving. I'll be here when you wake up."

Micah stood rooted beside his father until the gurney disappeared through a pair of doors then he made his way back to the waiting area. Tyler and Mary Lou looked up as he walked into the crowded space.

"How's George?" Tyler asked.

Micah said, "Telling me that if I don't close my mouth, I'll draw flies."

Mary Lou chuckled. "He's his usual quirky self, then."

"Pretty much."

Tyler's mom finished whatever she'd been doing on the phone and turned to Tyler and Micah. "I've got a few clients to meet today, including a prospect for a high-end horse farm that some doctor out of Dallas is interested in buying. But I'll be back this afternoon to check on everyone." She gave each of them a kiss, making Micah chuckle when she wiped the lipstick off their cheeks after each one.

After she'd disappeared, Micah and Tyler were quiet for several minutes before Tyler leaned close and patted Micah's thigh. "Everything will be fine. You'll see," Tyler said.

A warm buzz flowed from the spot he'd touched. Micah wanted to share something much more intimate but he knew this wasn't the right time. *Still, a man can wish for more, can't he?*

Morning slipped away while they messed with their phones and made inconsequential chit-chat. Tyler checked his watch and glanced at Micah. "We need to get lunch. What sounds good?"

Micah's stomach rumbled, but he shook his head when he turned to Tyler. "I don't think I could choke anything down, especially nothing from the hospital cafeteria. I guess I'll entertain myself."

"Okay. I'll be back in a bit."

The minutes dragged along since Micah had no one to help him pass the time. He wondered if Tyler had decided not to return when a delicious odor wafted past him. His stomach growled even louder than before. He glanced down the hall and a grinning Tyler had both hands filled with meals. He motioned Micah to a corner where a few tables were clustered. Once they'd found seats, Tyler divided the food and drinks between them. This time Micah's hunger wasn't in question. The food smelled delicious, and Tyler had surprised him by picking his favorites.

"You shouldn't have done this. I would have been fine," Micah said.

Tyler motioned toward the food. "It's no big deal. Now, eat."

They devoured the meals, and quicker than Micah thought possible, they were finishing the last of the onion rings. Tyler leaned back, burped then laughed. "Sorry. It was just too good."

Micah chuckled around a cheeseburger he was working on and found it was one of the best he'd had in a long time, either that or he'd been starving. As he ate, Tyler belched softly then turned red. "Sorry. That one got away."

Micah motioned him to silence. "Burp all you want. I appreciate you bringing back lunch, even if I said I didn't need it. I can't leave. If something happened, I would regret it for the rest of my life."

Tyler became thoughtful for a while before replying, "It's tough to be just the two of you. It's like you're the only support for the other person. I hope I'm making it easier."

"You are. I'm grateful you are here."

Tyler studied Micah then wiggled his eyebrows. "Oh? Any idea how you might reward me?"

Heat rolled over Micah's skin again but this time he refused to let Tyler get his goat. "I'm sure I can find a few ways to make you happy as hell."

"I guess I'll have to wait and see," Tyler said.

While he considered a response for Tyler's teasing, the volunteer appeared. "You're here with Mr. Vella?"

Micah swallowed hard and nodded. "Yes, I'm his son."

She pointed to a phone sitting on the table in the corner. "I'll transfer the surgical nurse to the phone beside you. Just pick it up when it rings."

Micah nodded, staring at the silent phone. A few seconds later it rang, and he almost jumped out of his seat but answered on the next ring.

"This is Micah Vella."

The nurse spent several minutes updating him on his father's condition. Once she'd given him a concise but professional rundown, Micah felt better. "So, everything is going well?" Micah asked.

"Yes, the doctor is being very thorough," she said, "but Mr. Vella should be in recovery in around an hour.

I'll call you again once the surgeon finishes to give you an update."

His nervous tension lessened somewhat as he considered every word she'd relayed to him as if she'd given him a legal brief.

"How's your dad?" Tyler asked when Micah hung up.

Micah started, having forgotten Tyler had only heard his side of the conversation. "Sorry. The surgery is going well. The doctor's double-checking everything but Dad should be in the recovery room in about an hour."

Tyler took Micah's hand in his and squeezed. "Sounds like things will be fine. Not much longer."

"Yeah, not too much longer."

Afternoon moved toward evening before the second call came, later than the hour Micah had been told. His concern had built from uneasy to worried as hell. When the news came, it took all his effort to focus on what he was being told. By the time the nurse had finished with the preliminary information, Micah narrowed down the gibberish going on in his head to two questions.

"What happened? Is he okay?"

His inquiries brought ominous silence. "There were some unexpected complications. Once Mr. Vella is in his room, the surgeon will come in and explain everything."

"But what about—"

The nurse cut Micah off. "I don't have any more information. Write down any questions you have so you don't forget them."

"But what...?" Micah realized he was listening to a dial tone. He stared at the phone then turned to Tyler.

"She wouldn't tell me what's wrong. She said the doctor would answer my questions."

Tyler's expression told Micah that neither of them were pleased about the way things were going. He hoped the outlook wasn't as grim as the nurse had left it. Tyler took him by the arm and guided them to a corner of the room that was more private. He kept his grip on Micah as they settled onto the seats. "Get yourself together. George doesn't need a single negative thought around him. He's going to beat this, but it will take work."

"Yeah, lots of work." Micah's desperation built.

Then Tyler took him by his jaw and turned Micah so they stared into each other's eyes. "You'll get help. Wait and see."

"Yeah. People will help," Micah said.

The next thing Micah knew, the hospital volunteer stood in from of them again. "They have Mr. Vella settled into his room. I can take you to see him."

Chapter Six

Tyler eased the saddle off Rusty and carted it to its rack in the trailer. He'd continued to have problems with his tack, and tonight had been no exception. As hard as he tried to fix the problem, the straps would be fine when he checked them just before the beginning of a ride, but by the time it ended, the cinch would be held together by nothing more than a few strands.

"It looked like you were having issues with your gear. Want me to check it over?" an unfamiliar voice said.

Stunned, Tyler stared at the bull rider standing beside him. He was about to ask why he'd want the guy's opinion when the unfamiliar cowboy began talking again.

"Sorry. I'm Dustin, Dustin Lewis. I'm on the bull-riding circuit and have seen you before. I noticed you're having issues with your saddle stuff and thought I'd offer to check it. You know…another set of eyes and all that junk." Dustin moved closer and dropped his voice. "My husband says I'm nosy and have no filter."

The declaration struck Tyler as funny and he chuckled. Before too long, the laughter built and had his legs weakening until he held onto the post to keep from collapsing. Dustin stood beside him grinning until Tyler had himself under control.

Tyler shook his head and sighed. "I don't mind you asking. The more help I get working out what's wrong, the more chances I have of finding the problem. If I nosedive off a horse at full gallop, it might be the accident I don't walk away from. So, I double- and triple-check everything before each round. So far, they've been fine at the beginning, but by the time it's over, the cinches look like I used an angle grinder on them. I'd love to solve the mystery. You want to see if you can figure out the issue?"

Dustin moved even closer but seemed uncomfortable. After a minute, he turned back. "Truth is I've never ridden a horse. Shane rides whenever he gets a chance, though. I can tell him the problems you're having and he might know what's wrong."

"Shane?" Tyler asked.

"The hubby. He's a bullfighter." He winked toward Tyler. "Shane hates being called the hubby, though, so that one will have to stay between us."

Tyler cocked his head and couldn't help but smile. The more he and Dustin talked, the more he recalled seeing Dustin ride. "You almost won last year's Nationals, right?"

"That was me. I'm making a second go at it this year. So far, so good."

Tyler nodded. "I thought you were high in the winnings."

Dustin shrugged. "It's going okay. Some of it's the luck of the draw. There are bulls who are mean and nasty but you gotta put in your eight seconds." Before Tyler could reply, Dustin had changed topics. "I gotta get ready. You don't win by getting bucked off." He'd disappeared into the crowd without Tyler understanding what he'd been talking about.

"Who was that, and what the hell was he jabbering about?"

Tyler glanced to see Everett appear from the crowd of people surrounding the gate. His hazer wore the smirk that Tyler had long ago decided was his normal demeanor. "He's one of the bull riders who's high in the rankings. He saw me checking my saddle and stopped to offer his help."

"And was he full of suggestions?"

"Not really. He doesn't ride horses, but he said his husband might know something."

Everett took in the information but kept silent. Tyler waited to see if he would say anything, but after a short wait, he resumed checking the last of his gear. He tugged on the final cinch and turned back to his partner. "Everything's fine. I guess we can watch the roping."

They headed to the fence when a familiar form separated from the crowd and headed toward them. *Micah*. They had been texting and burning up FaceTime, but it had been a few days since they'd been together. Tyler was glad to see the hot cowboy.

Micah launched himself at Tyler and the two shared a warm embrace. He let it go on for several seconds before they separated. The expression of happiness plastered across Micah's face brought a wash of pleasure to Tyler.

Before he could say anything, Everett held out his hand. "Give me your horse. You two might scare him. Don't be wandering off, though. We're up soon."

Tyler handed off the reins with a wink at Micah. He waited until Everett moved out of earshot before turning back and wrapping the rancher in another tight hug. Before the show of affection became awkward, he released Micah and stepped back. He wanted to carry him off somewhere so they could enjoy each other but that wouldn't happen.

Instead, he studied Micah as a flurry of questions flickered through his mind. He took a deep breath and began with the most important one. "How's your dad? Is he okay? Yesterday, you said the whole recovery thing was going slow. How were you able to leave?"

Micah motioned for Tyler to calm himself. "Dad's all right. As soon as he recovers from his surgery then they'll do more tests and see what treatments he needs. That should happen late this week or early next week. The waiting is about to kill me, but Dad keeps telling me I'm asking for trouble."

Tyler puckered his mouth and considered what to say next. He didn't want to be the meddling new…boyfriend? *I guess we aren't really at that point since we haven't had a real first date.* But before he started with a different line of questioning, Micah continued.

"He has other people coming over to help, too. His domino buddies are staying with him. And" — Micah winked at him — "your mom has been stopping by every day or two. She's the one who told me I should come see you."

Tyler became concerned. "I hope Mom didn't out you. She's real big on the whole gay son routine."

"No, we were outside. It was more like she was playing matchmaker." He chuckled at Tyler. "Your mommy likes me."

Tyler rolled his eyes and threw his hands up. "My mother is hopeless. She's been trying to find me a husband since I started college."

Micah chuckled. "That seems a little early to start the whole marriage thing."

"Okay, maybe she just wants me matched up with some cute guy. Marriage is a side effect of her main goal."

"And what's that?" Micah asked.

"Grandchildren."

Micah's gasp sent him into a fit of coughing that ended with Tyler pounding on his back. Once his choking spell stopped, he made random hand motions at Tyler as he fought to regain his speaking ability.

"Take a deep breath there, stud. It's *her* plan. I never said it was among my short-term goals. Breathe."

Micah wiped the tears from his eyes as his coughs turned into hysterical laughter. "That would be one way to break the news to my dad. 'George, your gay son and his husband are having twins.' That would put him into cardiac arrest."

Tyler considered Micah for a short while before rubbing his chin. "Do you really think he wouldn't understand?"

"Oh, hell, no. He needs to know but I can't get up the nerve to tell him. With all the health problems he's having right now, I don't want to add to his stress." Micah studied him before continuing. "You've been out since junior high, but I can't tell Dad. He won't take it well that his only child is gay. I hope you understand."

Tyler rested a hand on Micah's shoulder and shook his head. "I'm not trying to talk you into anything. Your coming out is yours. Just because I did it at thirteen doesn't mean you should have."

"Thanks for being cool about it," Micah said. "I'm working at it."

Tyler heard his name and saw Everett motioning to him. He turned back to Micah. "It's almost our round and Everett would shit himself if the routine got screwed up. After we're finished, dinner on me?"

"Sure." Micah gave Tyler a hug that hid a quick peck. The hidden display of affection rattled Tyler for a second but then he winked at Micah and hurried toward where Everett sat. He caught the reins swung to him and mounted the waiting horse. He tested his seat on the saddle and stood in the stirrups to confirm they were sound. Tyler dropped back and gave Everett a satisfied look. "It's fine. There shouldn't be any trouble tonight."

Everett smirked. "Good. I don't want you to cut into my pay."

"You keep the steer pointed the right direction and I'll do the rest."

The announcer helped entertain the spectators and keep them interested as they worked their way through the other steer wrestlers. There were quite a few before them, and by the time they reached Tyler, he was on edge and ready to do his run.

"Come on, cowboy. Let's win this thing," Everett said.

Tyler nodded, already narrowing his focus to the competition. He walked Rusty through the gate and moved into his box. He backed Rusty into the far corner so they would hit the barrier at a full gallop when their round started.

Once he was prepared, the tension cycled between him and his mount. He glanced over at Everett and got the nod indicating he was ready. Tyler did a final split-second check, nodded and the steer shot from the chute at a run.

His mount jumped through the barrier in pursuit of the five-hundred pounds of calf doing its best to escape. Tyler's heart pounded as he leaned along Rusty's outstretched neck. As he shifted his center of balance, something seemed off but this time he was too far committed for the shift to do more than create a tiny bobble in his long-practiced routine. He threw himself from the pounding horse and wrapped his arms around the steer's horns. A split-second later, he swung his legs forward and dug the heels of his boots into the powder-fine dirt of the arena.

Tyler reached familiar territory. His control wasn't what he would have liked, but it remained good enough that he might win this bulldogging event. He twisted the horns back with all his strength, and a long second later, all four of the steer's hooves flew into the air. Tyler held it for another few seconds before releasing him.

The animal jumped to its feet, trotted to the end of the arena and out the gate without a sign he'd been through any ordeal. Tyler walked toward the arena gate, knocking the dust from his clothes. He'd almost reached the exit when Everett rode beside him and held out the reins to Tyler's horse.

"Not bad. With the two previous rounds, you might place in the money."

Tyler chuckled before shaking his head at Everett. "All right, Eeyore. We won the whole thing and I plan to have a hell of a celebration tonight."

Everett rolled his eyes and shifted his grip on his own horse, which was becoming restless. "Have your party. I'll check in with you at the next rodeo."

"Yeah, a few more days and I'm off for a hell of a long trip to Montana."

Everett turned without another peep and disappeared into the crowd.

"Isn't he a little ray of sunshine?"

Tyler glanced over his shoulder at Micah. "That's normal for him. He always sounds like someone peed in his Post Toasties. But he's a damn good hazer, and he's the one who does all the organizing. It makes my life easier and him happier." Tyler took Micah by the shoulders. "Regardless of that cheerful thought, I won the steer wrestling, and I'm sure I promised you a dinner. How do you come down on grilled T-bone?"

Micah patted his stomach. "I love steak! I grew up on a ranch in Oklahoma. I'm not allowed to make any other choice."

Tyler considered his options but Micah's phone rang before he could reply. Micah studied the screen for a second before answering.

"Hey, what's up?"

Tyler's nerves eased when Micah winked at him before going back to the one-sided conversation. "If that's what he wants, I don't see a reason for him not to have it."

After a few more single word responses, the talk was ending. "He's kind of cantankerous sometimes. Call whenever you have questions."

Micah ended the conversation about to burst with laughter. The sound from him was like a rusty old hinge in need of oil. After a few more strange noises, Micah caught his breath and explained.

"That was Kenny. Since that first day when Dad showed him how to garden, they've been the best of buddies. He comes and does whatever Lee has for him then helps Dad the rest of the day. He's getting into the whole farming and ranching thing. Dad loves it. He always liked to teach."

"So, why'd he call—and so late? I thought your dad's friends were sitting with him."

"Which would be the funny part. Dad's been keeping the domino buddies updated about Kenny, so they invited him to play with them tonight. But now Dad's decided he wants a bowl of ice cream."

"Okay…"

"Kenny is the designated driver for the group."

"So, they have the kid calling you for permission to eat ice cream?"

"Pretty much," Micah said.

Tyler covered his face and laughed. A few minutes later, they regained control of themselves, and with a final hissing gasp, turned to each other. "Well, since Kenny has the old wankers mastered, we can enjoy a good steak." He hesitated for a second and smacked his hands against his jeans so the arena dust came off in tiny clouds. "I need to clean up. Wrestling with a wiry steer in the dirt doesn't keep me spotless."

"No problem. But let's get going before my stomach starts growling."

Tyler nodded in agreement and motioned in the general direction of his rig. They were both quiet until they were inside the living space and Tyler began stripping. It didn't take long for him to realize that Micah had locked his gaze onto his bare chest. He grinned at Micah's bright red face. "See something you like?"

Tyler hadn't thought it was possible for Micah to turn more crimson, but he almost matched a roaring bonfire. He snorted a little before meeting Tyler's gaze. "No use lying about it, I guess. I was enjoying the show."

Tyler kicked off his boots, opened his jeans and let them drop to his ankles. Once he had stripped to a pair of charcoal-gray briefs, he winked again. "How about now? See anything you like?"

"You're an evil shit," Micah said.

Tyler closed the gap between the two of them, ran his hands over Micah's back and pressed their lips together. They separated a short time later with both of them panting.

"And now?" Tyler asked.

Micah nodded as he swallowed hard a few times. He grabbed Tyler by the shoulders, spun him around and pushed him toward the tiny shower. "Get washed up or we'll never make it to the steak place."

Tyler shot Micah a lecherous grin as he peeled off his underwear and kicked them onto a pile of clothes laying in the corner. He kept any other comments to himself as he tugged the plastic curtain closed and began cleaning up for their evening. It only took a few minutes before the last of the suds circled the drain. He opened the shower and wiped the water from his eyes. "Hey, hand me a towel, please. They're in the cabinet outside the door."

Micah walked to the storage that Tyler had pointed at, lifted out a towel stacked there and handed it to him. He dried off what he could inside the tiny shower before stepping out to finish. He didn't tease Micah any further for fear he would combust, but he wasn't bashful about showing off. With a final pass of the plush cloth between his legs, Tyler tossed it onto the pile of clothes.

After a few more minutes of Tyler displaying the goods, Micah cleared his throat. "Get something on or I'm not responsible for my actions."

Tyler shook his dick at Micah. "You mean you want some of this?"

Micah chuckled. "I wanted steak, not sausage. Now, quit showing off and get dressed."

"But later?"

"We'll see how good you are at picking out places to eat."

Tyler took out a pair of dark red briefs and considered for a moment before tossing them back into the drawer. He winked at Micah as he tugged on his jeans and buttoned them. "Yeah, whatever. But I'm getting hungry, too, so I'll let it go."

Tyler decided he'd teased Micah enough, and besides, he was starved. It didn't take him long before he was threading a hand-tooled belt through his jeans and stomping his boots to be certain they were all the way on. He turned to Micah. "How's this?"

"You look good enough to eat."

Tyler wrapped his arms around Micah's waist and pulled him in for another kiss. "We better go. I'm starved and you're what I really want to eat."

Chapter Seven

The trip to the restaurant didn't take long since Tyler had picked one of his favorites close to the fairgrounds. He rolled to a stop, bailed from the pickup and made his way to the passenger side. Before Micah had time to react, Tyler opened the door and motioned for him to exit.

"Your dining experience awaits you, handsome prince."

"Oh, Lord," Micah muttered as they walked to the entrance.

Tyler reached over and placed his hand in the small of Micah's back. His eyes grew wide from Tyler's touch and he glanced over. "Not that I don't like it, but do we want to be that blatant with the PDAs?"

"You're hot, and everyone will be jealous that you're with me. They can suck it up and get over it."

Micah studied him for a little while before he shrugged. "You're the one who knows this place. I'll trust your judgment."

Tyler ran his arm around Micah's waist and drew him closer. "You should trust my judgment on everything."

Micah snorted and seemed about to say something, but they had reached the entrance. Tyler let his hand slip off so he could open the door for Micah. He stepped inside and shot the host his most charming smile. It did what Tyler hoped and got the young man flustered, but it also got them a great table in a quiet corner. He surveyed the room while the waiter took their drink orders and disappeared into the sea of dim lights and murmured conversations, all of which gave Tyler time to focus on Micah. He was a little shocked at the expression on Micah's face. The lifted eyebrow and smirk were not what he'd expected.

"What's up?"

"Do you always get your way by flirting?"

The accusation surprised Tyler. "What're you talking about? I wasn't flirting with anyone. I wouldn't even know how to do it."

"A hundred-watt smile and a wink are a good start."

"That's not flirting! I was just being friendly."

Micah patted Tyler's hand and chuckled. "I'm teasing. So long as it doesn't go too far, I don't mind. But I'm not real big on sharing."

Tyler would have said more but he felt like they were being watched. He did a careful check of the room and everything appeared normal. He guessed it wasn't anything but the conversation he'd been having with Micah.

The rest of the evening went well from Tyler's perspective. The food was delicious and he enjoyed talking with Micah. He also tried to dial down the friendly cowboy routine. He may have meant nothing by his actions, but if it bothered Micah enough for him to say something, then it was worth the effort to tone it down.

Micah finished the last of his meal and slumped against the seat. "You get to pick where we eat next time, too. This was one of the best meals I've ever had."

A warm sense of accomplishment filled Tyler. "Glad to hear it." He tuned up his smile again but this time he directed it at Micah. "I like the dessert here, but I made something sweet this morning that I think you'll like."

Micah's eyes twinkled as he stared at Tyler. "Sounds delicious."

It didn't take long before they headed out the door and walked toward Tyler's truck. He had the same sensation of being watched, but this time when he scanned the surrounding area, he knew why. A guy not much older than Micah was charging toward them with two other men close behind.

"Nutcase at three o'clock. He has two wingmen," Tyler said. He understood from experience what this trio wanted. He and Micah would hear the recent rants from the representatives of the local homophobes. It relieved Tyler when he couldn't spot any clubs or bats, but that realization was only faint comfort in a country returning to the lawless Wild West. But he would wait and see how bad it was.

The trio slowed as they got within a few yards of Tyler and Micah before coming to a stop. It gave Tyler a thread of hope that they hadn't rushed them. He could tell the guys approaching them were working up their courage for whatever they had in mind. Tyler had dealt with people like this a few times in the past, but his size had deterred most of the thugs. From the expressions on these men, they wouldn't be that easy. They appeared to have poured down enough liquid courage to decide Tyler and Micah would want to hear their opinions.

"Hey, you two!"

Tyler squared up as the obvious ringleader stepped closer, but he kept his silence to see what the guy might do. He'd moved so he could protect Micah. That lasted all of two seconds before Micah shifted to his side. Tyler read the determination on Micah's face.

"Y'all need to get outta here. We don't want your kind in our town."

"Why? Afraid someone might realize your cumulative IQ is less than the speed limit through town?" Tyler said.

They hesitated for a moment before scowling at the pair. Instead of attacking, they hovered near each other and yelled taunts at Tyler and Micah. After a few minutes, Tyler grew tired of the posturing and threats. "What are you doing? This shit is getting old."

"Damn queers!" the leader yelled and ran at Tyler with another guy close behind. One of them peeled off and sprinted toward Micah. The thugs were closing the distance and Tyler readied himself. The leader ran full speed at Tyler with his arm cocked for a powerful punch. By this time, his expression twisted and the air filled with his obscenities.

At the last instant, Tyler stepped in and shot out a well-timed jab. There was a satisfying crunch when he landed his fist on the attacker's jaw. He studied Tyler with shock etched across his face. A second later, his eyes rolled back and he crumbled into a gasping pile on the blacktop.

He sensed another attack coming and dropped to his knee. The air a handbreadth above him hissed as the second attacker swung his arm through the vacated space. As he readied for a second punch, Tyler realized his assailant held a knife and seemed ready to carve him into pieces. *Oh! Is this the way you want to play this game? Let's see what you've got.*

Tyler coiled his muscles, and with the power he used to toss a five-hundred-pound steer to the ground, he lunged forward. He threw an upper cut so low that it caught his assailant in the balls. A scream of agony filled the night. The attacker crumbled to the ground, moaning and clutching his crotch with both hands. Tyler kicked the knife far out of reach.

The second his attackers were out, Tyler spun to give Micah a hand. But when he did, he found Micah sitting on the middle of the third attacker's back. From what Tyler could tell, the man was out cold, but Micah had an arm lock on him that would keep him immobilized.

"I'd ask if you need any help, but you seem to have everything under control," Tyler said.

Micah pushed harder against the arm trapped beneath him. "Apparently, all those years of martial arts were useful."

"We can take over for you, unless you're having too much fun."

Tyler glanced over to see two uniformed police officers standing to the side, watching he and Micah with intensity.

"We'd be happy to let you take charge. These three jumped us and one of them was carrying a knife."

"That's the story we got from the restaurant manager, too. They called nine-one-one when the little scuffle started. We wanted to make sure no one was hurt." He studied first Tyler then Micah. "You boys carrying any weapons?"

Tyler struggled with the odd way things were developing, but Micah moved beside him and patted Tyler on the shoulder before turning to the cop. "All we have in our pockets are keys, wallets and phones. These three jumped us with no reason."

Tyler considered what he should add, but then Micah bumped the back of his hand. He had the distinct impression it was something important, but he needed time to work it out. It gave him enough hesitation to let Micah continue talking with the cops.

"Whatever we need to do, we want to file charges against these guys. From what they yelled at us, this is a hate crime. No way are we going to leave that for someone else to deal with."

The officers glanced at each other before taking statements from Micah and Tyler, but they were obviously not happy about being forced to file a report. Micah watched everything that transpired closely, and he obviously wasn't pleased with what he saw. He even had to ask for copies of the reports. By that time, Tyler understood that this wasn't going the way it should and he became as guarded as Micah.

After an extraordinary amount of time, the cops left with the attackers tucked into the back seat. Through the entire situation, they had treated Tyler and Micah more like criminals than victims. Once they headed back to the pickup, Tyler felt uneasy and ready to be anywhere else. He braced himself when he saw the manager coming toward them with a grim expression.

"Hi, guys. Sorry about all that. Normally we have a peaceful town. Safe, you know?"

"Sure," Tyler said. "We get that. It wasn't us that started the trouble tonight."

"Oh, I know. I wasn't blaming you. But I wanted you to know that the guy whose jaw you broke? He's the brother of one of the cops and best friend to the other. If you're passing through, cut your visit short."

Tyler turned to Micah. "How do you feel about helping me move everything to the next rodeo?"

Micah stared in the direction the police car had gone then back to Tyler. "I'll follow. If there's anything to haul, we can throw it into my pickup."

Tyler glanced first at Micah then the Good Samaritan. Neither of them were at all happy about the way things were shaping up. He wasn't pleased that it seemed like he was running. Tyler never liked feeling as if he had taken the coward's way out. This was one of those times when he needed to be cautious or he and Micah might be the latest police harassment story to make the national news. The nervous behavior of the manager alone gave him enough reason not to challenge the situation.

After convincing himself that leaving would be the most prudent choice, he nodded toward Micah. "Let's head out. If you're okay to help, we can be at the next rodeo in a few hours."

Micah raced around the truck and climbed into the passenger seat before Tyler opened the door. By the time they reached the trailer and Micah's pickup, Tyler's nerves were as taut as guitar strings. Things became frantic while they were getting the horse and equipment ready to leave. But in what seemed to be only seconds, they were driving from the fairgrounds. Tyler kept checking that Micah remained behind him. His heart pounded as their little caravan threaded its way off the grounds and toward the interstate.

The knot in Tyler's gut unraveled when the city limits were in his rear-view mirror and the grill of Micah's pickup was close behind him. Tyler had been on the rodeo circuit since he had been in junior high and he'd been out about being gay for much of it. Some people used it as a reason to spout off homophobic crap, but no one had attacked him before and he'd sure as hell never gotten a knife pulled on him. Then to have the cops maneuvering against him? The combination left him shaken.

Not too many miles later, they swung onto the interstate and headed southwest. Tyler hoped today's trouble stayed far behind him. Other than a stop for gasoline and something to drink, the trip was uneventful. Soon, they arrived at their destination and had the rig settled into a parking spot. He climbed out of the pickup and walked back to Micah.

"Any problems?"

"Nope. It ended up being a nice, easy trip." Micah glanced around before returning to Tyler. "I have to say that I don't mind being a hundred miles from that whole pile of crazy."

"I agree. Let's get everything situated and we can relax a little."

Micah nodded in agreement, "I'll get the trailer unhooked and you take care of Rusty. It shouldn't take much time."

They flew into the work. As Micah had predicted, it didn't take long before they were relaxing on the loveseat. Tyler had taken off his boots and socks before he curled against the end. "What a crazy night. It still kind of feels like I let them win, though."

Micah shook his head before twisting and putting his feet on Tyler. "You didn't run from anyone. It was a stacked deck, so stop sweating over it. But I have one thing you can worry about."

Tendrils of doubt wound their way through Tyler as he worried what he'd done wrong. "What's that?"

"I have boots and socks that need taking off. My tootsies are getting tired and need to breathe."

The worries disappeared like a puff of smoke on a windy day and Tyler grinned. "That I can do." Tyler worked a boot until it slipped over Micah's heel and he tossed it into the same pile as his own. In a few minutes, he'd repeated the process and had Micah's bare feet in his lap. He reached over, took one foot in his hand and started giving Micah a foot rub.

As he recalled the day, one thing nagged at him and it was not going to disappear. He slowed at his task then stopped and Micah focused on him.

"What's up?" Micah asked.

Tyler shook his head and resumed his foot rub. "Nothing. Just me zoning off."

Micah grabbed his wrist and stopped Tyler. "Tell me. We can't keep things from each other."

Tyler tensed, blowing air through his teeth. "I don't suppose I could get a Mulligan?"

"Nope. What's going on?"

"Okay, fine. But remember you insisted."

"Spit it out."

Tyler nodded. "I was a little surprised. When those guys jumped us, I thought you'd bug out."

Micah sat up and tucked his feet back under his butt. He studied Tyler for a few seconds before speaking. "Why? Did you really think I'd be such a chickenshit?"

"No! It wasn't that at all. I'm not explaining this right."

"Give it another shot. You get more tries," Micah said.

Tyler moved his hands in random patterns as his panic built. "Okay. You aren't out to George. I get that. I didn't think you'd want him to find out by hearing you were part of a gay couple who had been attacked. That's why I worried."

Micah stared at Tyler and the tension grew then Micah dropped his gaze to the floor and slumped against the couch. They remained like that for a considerable time. Tyler was close to breaking the long silence when Micah spoke.

"I know at some point I'll have to tell him, but I can't find the right time or the courage. I love my dad but he's real old-school and religious. I'm afraid that it would kill him to find out his only son has the hots for other dudes."

Tyler twisted his lips as he considered Micah's explanation. But as he tested the idea, he found it difficult to understand. "I can't imagine George not accepting you. He's a great guy. He knows I'm gay and doesn't care."

"But you aren't his child. I'm not saying he'll go bonkers and try to kill me or something, but I can imagine the disappointment that would be on his face every time he looked at me."

"So, why didn't you run? Otherwise, he might find out."

"I'm not sure. It never occurred to me to leave you to face those guys by yourself."

Tyler tugged Micah's bare feet to him again and began rubbing them as he considered what had been said. It didn't take long for the sentiment to soak into him. "I wasn't trying to tell you how to live your life. I guess I was being nosy more than anything else. Sorry if I made you uncomfortable."

Micah wiggled back into the pillows on the couch and the tension lessened. He stared at the ceiling for a moment before speaking. "You didn't make me uncomfortable, and I appreciate the support. It's just that my dad has enough crap going on these days, and like I've said before, I can't bring myself to set him up to deal with any more stress."

Tyler nodded but kept his silence. He had already asked too many questions — most of which were none of his business. But then Micah sighed. "You give a damn good foot rub. It's amazing."

Glad the topic had changed, Tyler motioned to Micah. "We could watch a movie. I really did make dessert." He looked a little sheepish. "I was feeling homesick. But it's ready if you're still interested."

Micah studied him for a few seconds before cocking his head and giving Tyler a shy glance. "I don't suppose it has anything to do with chocolate?"

"Chocolate pecan pie."

Micah smacked his lips. "With ice cream?"

"Of course."

"Then the answer is a hungry 'yes'."

Tyler winked and untwined himself from their nest. He dished up a dessert for each of them, settled onto the seat beside Micah and handed him a bowl. "Try it. It's a slight variation on a family recipe."

One of Micah's brows shot up as he studied Tyler then the treat. "You made it?"

Tyler chuckled and waved his spoon at him. "Yes, I cooked it. Don't be so surprised." He bit into the mixture and moaned. A few seconds later, he filled his spoon with another bite and offered it to Micah. "Try it. I promise you won't be disappointed."

Micah looked at the offered tidbit and shrugged. He leaned forward and took the morsel. Micah slowly chewed but when he swallowed, his face was infused with happiness. "That's wonderful. Sweet, with a bite in the chocolate. Does it have some chili in it?"

Tyler chuckled, delighted Micah enjoyed the dessert. "Yes, a touch of cayenne."

"Well, it's amazing." Micah scooted close, and offered a spoonful to Tyler. His stomach fluttered at the inadvertent touch against Micah's cheek. The heat of desire that had been burning low since they'd arrived built in intensity. He responded to Micah's sharing and offered him a spoonful. When he did, a drop of chocolate landed just below his lip.

Tyler caught the drip on his fingertip and held it out. He sighed when Micah took the finger between his lips and nursed it. The tingle of pleasure rushed through Tyler, leaving him with a hard cock and gasping for air. When Micah let Tyler slip free, their gazes met and they smiled at each other.

"That blew my mind, especially your final cleanup maneuver," Tyler said.

With an expression of devilry on his face, Micah ran his finger through the last of the syrup, leaned close and coated Tyler's lips. He moved lower until their mouths touched, and this time excitement crackled through Tyler. He set their empty plates out of the way before turning back to Micah. He ran his hands over Micah, drawing the shorter man closer until they were lying on each other. With the chocolate gone, the kiss changed into pure passion and the gentle pleasure became jolts of sexual excitement that flowed over Tyler.

He slipped his hands over Micah's tight body, kissing down his chest as he opened his shirt a button at a time. He pushed the clothing over Micah's shoulder and let it flutter to the floor then wrapped his arms around Micah and kissed down his neck until he squirmed with arousal. Tyler moved lower and reached the circle of short, dark hair surrounding Micah's navel. He ran his tongue through the outcropping as his senses filled with the masculine tastes and smells of the man under him.

He sat up and relished the sensation of Micah's hard cock wedged between his butt cheeks. "How's that? Any complaints?"

Micah groaned and shook his head as he unbuttoned the bottom few snaps of Tyler's shirt and ran his hands over Tyler's chest. The touch left trails of fire that brought Tyler to new levels of desire. "It's feeling amazing for me. Now, it's my turn," Tyler said.

Micah nodded in agreement but kept his silence. He untangled himself from Tyler, pushed him against the couch then spent a few minutes rubbing Tyler's feet. Tyler enjoyed the attention more than he might have ever expected. When he looked up, Micah stood, motioning him to stand. Tyler lifted his eyebrows and Micah chuckled.

"Come on, big boy. For what I have in mind for tonight, you don't need clothes."

A shudder of anticipation cracked through Tyler's body. He eagerly followed Micah's instructions and stood before the sexy rancher. He had no doubt the lump in his jeans would tell Micah how horny he was. As Micah opened the first button, Tyler sighed with anticipation. His decision to go commando became obvious when his bush came into view. Afraid his throbbing dick wouldn't last through any more of Micah's teasing, he reached down and finished opening his jeans with a couple of tugs. His dick swung free of the cloth, trailing a wet strand from its tip.

Micah looked at it and licked his lips. "Holy fuck."

Tyler chuckled. "I try not to disappoint."

"I want you out of the rest of your clothes...right now." Micah started pulling and tugging until he had Tyler stripped.

Tyler felt more self-conscious than normal. He knew he didn't fit the dream gay man look. Micah seemed to think he was hot, though, and that was enough. The twinkle in Micah's eyes said everything Tyler wanted to hear. As he began to refocus, he realized Micah had stripped and was stroking himself. The expression he shot Tyler was pure lust, and Tyler couldn't be more okay with how things were going.

Micah took the tip of Tyler's hard cock into his mouth and began running his tongue around the head. Tyler's muscles turned to goo. A few seconds later, Tyler rested his hands on Micah's shoulder to keep from collapsing. He enjoyed the exquisite agony but didn't want the pleasure to end so quickly. He lifted Micah to his feet and moved in for a lingering kiss.

"That is amazing, but if you keep it up, I'm going to shoot my load and we'll be done."

"And that would be bad?" Micah asked with a smirk.

Tyler's smile stretched from ear to ear. "I thought if we lasted a little longer, that might be good."

"And what did you have in mind?" Micah asked.

"Well, I do have a huge bed in this thing."

Without a word, Micah scrambled up the stairs and Tyler heard the thump when he launched himself across the queen-size bed. Tyler followed him up the short flight of stairs to find Micah sprawled across the mattress, stroking himself. Without hesitation, Tyler crawled between Micah's legs and worked his way inch-by-inch up his body as Micah worked his cock.

Micah trembled when Tyler pressed his face under his balls and inhaled. Tyler's senses were buried with the smell and taste of sex and man. Micah muttered something incoherent when Tyler ran his tongue over one of his balls. With Micah's legs on his shoulders, he enjoyed exploring while Micah writhed on the bed. He moved back and pried open Micah's ass to find his tight hole twitching. Hungry for more of this man, Tyler dove and explored his entrance. Soon he drove the end of his tongue into Micah. His head spun as he relished the scents and sensations surrounding them. Micah squirmed, his moans increasing in volume as Tyler readied him for what they both wanted next.

Micah pulled his legs higher, opening himself to Tyler's attention. They explored each other until Tyler pulled back and enjoyed the sight of Micah lost in the pleasure Tyler had given him. He sprawled across the bed and pulled the condoms and lube from a drawer. He turned to Micah, holding out the needed supplies.

"Ready?"

Micah's body was coated with a fine sheen of sweat and a look of sexual hunger lived in his eyes. "Fuck me. Oh, hell. Don't tease me more."

Tyler gave him a searing look as he rolled the condom down his cock and coated it with lube. He moved close, kissed Micah's hip then slipped a slick finger into his ass. He eased his finger deeper as Micah froze with his mouth hanging open. Tyler worked his finger slowly inside Micah until its entire length was buried. Micah was obviously lost in the sensations and Tyler knew it was time.

He moved between Micah's legs until the head of his cock kissed Micah's wet hole. He paused for a second before beginning to press forward. The tight heat around his dick felt amazing and Micah's groans of pleasure drove him onward. He moved deeper inside until his bush ground against Micah's butt.

"Oh, fuck," Micah moaned. "That feels amazing."

Tyler eased almost out. "Just wait... This is only the beginning."

He pushed Micah's legs higher and started driving inside. Soon, they were lost in the all-encompassing lovemaking. Gasping for breath, Tyler sank deeper in their passion as he pounded Micah's ass. He'd lost all track of time when he felt Micah tremble under him as the first volley of Micah's orgasm shot between them. Micah grabbed his cock and jerked it while he sprayed both of them with hot cum.

With each thrust, Micah's ass clamped around Tyler's dick, taking him closer. A few strokes later, the lightning storm of euphoria signaled that Tyler had reached his climax. He buried himself inside Micah as his body enjoyed wave after wave of pleasure.

Exhausted and satisfied, Tyler sank on top of Micah and gave him a slow, sensuous kiss. They held each other tight, working to calm themselves. Micah pulled Tyler close and sighed. "That was amazing. I feel like my whole body is jelly."

Tyler ran his hand over Micah, enjoying the sensation of touching his body. The time passed slowly, but when Tyler's softening cock slipped from inside, he eased himself onto the bed beside Micah. Tyler disposed of the condom, retrieved a wash cloth and set about cleaning off the evidence of their lovemaking. Once he'd finished, he crawled back beside Micah and spooned. With a last kiss, his eyes twinkled. "Would you like to spend the night?"

Micah winked and smacked Tyler on the ass. "A sleepover would be fun."

They crawled into bed together and Tyler knew the single round of enjoyment wouldn't last either of them through the night. True to his intuition, their final session ended with dawn only hours away.

The next conscious thought from Tyler was a phone demanding attention. Still only half awake, he fumbled for his cell. But before he could locate it, Micah had answered the noisy beast.

"Hey, Dad. Everything okay?"

Micah's face became grim as he listened. His conversation with his father was short, which Tyler took to be a bad sign. But he understood what needed to happen.

"Grab your stuff. I'll help you get out of here as quick as possible," he said.

Chapter Eight

Micah drove down the gravel road to the ranch at a speed only a rollercoaster addict would be comfortable with. His dad had sounded too composed on the phone. Micah recognized the tone of voice that told him how serious the situation had become. The hours since he'd left Tyler had done nothing to decrease the tension from his dad's call. That his father had told him he didn't have to come to the doctor with him was an embarrassment for Micah. George had worried about ruining Micah's fun. That his dad thought he needed to tell him that? Well, they'd talk about that later.

His pickup fishtailed around a sharp turn and traveled sideways down the road until he got the truck under control. He chided himself. He had to get there in one piece or he wouldn't be any help. Micah focused on finishing the final miles left in the trip.

He made the last curve and the familiar sight relieved him. Micah eased in at a normal speed. His dad would tell him what he thought of Micah taking risks to get home a little quicker. As he rolled to a stop before the front gate, he jumped from the truck, raced up the sidewalk and sprinted for the front door.

Grabbing the knob, he turned it under his hand. He paused as the door opened to his dad standing framed in the entryway. The glint in George's eye let him know he was busted.

"I told you I could go by myself. If I'd known you'd driven to the next rodeo, I wouldn't have phoned you at all."

Cold dread filled Micah. "Dad, I want to be with you. Please don't cut me out because you don't want to bother me."

George sighed and lifted a brow at Micah. "I know. That's why I called. Go clean up. I made you a sandwich. We need to leave in about an hour."

Micah nodded and dodged into the house with no other discussion. He found a change of clothes laid out on his bed and had to grin at his dad still picking out what he'd wear. But there was no use trying to get George to do anything different. Mentioning it wouldn't change anything, but it would piss off his dad.

He moved to get ready and stripped. As Micah peeled off the last of the clothing, there was the distinct odor of the sex he and Tyler had shared. *Dad called that one. I would have reeked all day.* He balanced first on one foot then the other as he yanked off his socks. He trotted to the bathroom, climbed into the shower and washed himself. In only a few short minutes, he'd finished and walked back into the room, drying his hair. He tossed the damp towel onto the basket of dirty laundry then slipped on the clean clothes. He was pulling on his boots when there was a knock at his bedroom door.

"You about ready? I don't want to be rushed," George said.

An almost silent chuckle leaked from Micah. Dad's idea of prompt was fifteen minutes early. He was sure some people adjusted the time they invited him to an event to keep him from showing up too early. Micah recognized his father's MO from years of dealing with him. He popped the last boot onto his foot and trotted over to open the door, finding his father poised to knock again.

"I'm ready. Let's go. I know how you hate to be late."

George patted Micah on the shoulder and turned without another word. Micah followed behind and they made for the truck. Neither of them were very talkative. Micah glanced over to find his dad staring straight ahead, deep in thought. He could understand the sentiment and echoed it as they headed for the interstate.

The trip to the doctor's office seemed brief to Micah. Parking was a challenge, but they arrived well before the time of the appointment. He sat down in the reception area while his dad checked in. He held in a chuckle when his dad sat beside him and leaned close.

"The lady at the desk said it might be a few minutes. We're a little early."

"No problem. It'll give me a chance to check my email."

"You're welded to that thing. You'd think it was your lifeline."

This was a familiar refrain between the two of them, one Micah saw no reason to take part in except for a few strategic grunts and an occasional 'uh-huh'. A few minutes later, his dad picked up an outdoor magazine and settled in to read while Micah flipped through the emails he had on his phone. After erasing a handful of junk ones, he spotted what he'd been hoping he would have — a message from Tyler.

Just seeing Tyler's name on the list had him excited. He opened it with a quick tap then scanned the note. It was short. Tyler's messages were never chatty. You'd think he kept it to the hundred-and-forty-character limit on everything. Still, Micah found it heartwarming.

Hey, Stud!
Sorry you had to leave early. Next time, I'll make you breakfast.
Let me know what the doc says about George. I'm happy to help any way you need me.
Take care,
Tyler

Sure, it was short. *But he hit all the points. Last night was a blast. Keep him posted on Dad's condition, and if there is a way for him to help, let him know. Short, sweet and to the point. Typical Tyler.*

"Any hot notes?"

He rolled his eyes and blanked the screen before turning to his dad. "Just Tyler checking on you and telling me they're happy to help if we need anything."

"You and the Lang boy have become tight over the past month or so," said George.

Micah jerked in surprise at his question. He considered how he should respond and decided the truth was best — but not the whole, unvarnished truth. "We're more at similar stages in our lives now. He's a nice guy and I enjoy hanging around with him."

George was clearly considering his reply when the nurse called his name. They followed her into the catacombs of the offices where she took all the measurements invented by mankind and left them in one of the tiny exam rooms. To Micah's relief, George didn't bring up the conversation they'd been having. They sat in the room and George made observations about the various jars of supplies and equipment until Micah needed a break. At that point, there was a knock and the doctor appeared. He moved to the counter and put his computer on it. He read the information in silence before turning toward the two of them and gave them a somber greeting.

"I asked you to come in to go over the results of your recent CT scan."

"I'm guessing they aren't going to make me happy," George said.

"Some parts of the scan are less conclusive than I would like. I want to proceed with more aggressive treatment."

"More chemo?" George asked.

"Yes…and radiation."

"How bad are the side effects going to be this time?"

The doctor studied George then glanced at Micah before turning back to address George's question. "They vary from patient to patient. Some people's reactions become more severe as treatment progresses, while they stay mild in others."

"What would you recommend?" Micah asked.

This time the oncologist narrowed his focus to Micah. "That you do whatever it takes to make your father comfortable."

George held up a hand to forestall Micah and turned to the physician. "I've changed my mind from my first reaction before. Now I want to fight this thing—for me and my son."

"When will he be starting the therapy?" Micah asked.

Silence hung in the room while the doctor worked at the screen. Micah came close to repeating his question before he looked up. "The nurse will set up the first treatment today. It's best we start them as soon as possible but it would be up to Mr. Vella."

Cold tendrils of fear twisted their way through Micah. He knew if they were starting chemo this fast that the situation was likely dire. Micah also wasn't certain his dad would agree to more aggressive treatment, in spite of what he'd said. He was becoming overwhelmed when his dad squeezed Micah's shoulder.

George said, "If that's what you think is best, we can start everything today."

It surprised Micah that his dad had become so accommodating. That alone told him how serious George was about the situation. A knot formed in Micah's stomach as he struggled with his despair. He was already drowning in a flood of loss. Micah barely remembered his mother before breast cancer had taken her. He'd been too young to understand what had happened, but he'd always remember his dad's tears.

Since then, it had only been the two of them. Now, Micah wasn't sure how he would deal with being alone. He glanced at his dad again. He'd have to be the support for his dad that his father had always been for him. He nodded and patted George on the shoulder before turning to the doctor. "Whatever we need to do. Starting today sounds like a positive first step."

The next few hours were a whirl of activities as nurses came through on a routine basis, preparing George. The schedule overwhelmed Micah, but he hid that from his dad. Eventually, they were in the treatment waiting room. George sat reading yet another outdoor magazine. Micah spent the time trying to distract himself by playing with every app on his phone.

It buzzed and writhed in his hands and he almost dropped it. He grabbed it as the device broke into its dance again. "Damn it."

"Micah, your language," George said with a lifted brow.

He glanced over to his dad. "Sorry. The little creature startled me."

George shook his head and went back to his magazine. Micah glanced at his screen to see who had texted him. His face turned into a grin when he saw it was Tyler.

How's it going?

Micah tried to calm himself. He had no right to dump all the bad news on Tyler. He had to be the one to help his dad, and he would do it without assistance.

It's going okay. Waiting. You know how hospitals are.

The pause that resulted stretched out long enough that he thought Tyler'd finished. But the typing indicator started again and Micah knew he hadn't escaped. His tension grew with each passing second until the message popped into existence.

You stayed for treatment. How bad is it?

Micah wasn't surprised he'd been busted. Tyler picked up on personal issues. It was useless to avoid the conversation. Tyler would ferret out the gory details. Micah gave him the truth but saw no reason to speculate.

The cancer's still there. The doc said to wait until after treatment and he'd look at it again.

This time the reply shot back.

You need help?

Micah's response was just as fast.

No. I got this.

If you need help and don't tell me...

He decided this conversation needed to stop.

They're calling for Dad. Gotta go.

'K. Love you.

The 'love you' rattled Micah, but he didn't have a clue how to reply. He wasn't sure he was ready to go into the 'L' zone. Still panicking, the call came for George, and Micah left without a reply to Tyler. Micah found himself embarrassed to leave Tyler hanging, but a minute passed and as the needle slid into his dad's vein, the seriousness settled onto Micah. He collapsed into the chair beside his dad, trying to control his emotions. When he regarded his father again, it was obvious the gravity of the situation had struck him, too.

Micah decided the only thing he could do at this point was try to make George as comfortable as possible.

Over the next few hours, he asked the questions his dad was too nice to pepper the oncology nurses with.

At first, George acted okay, but when they unhooked him and deemed him ready to leave, it couldn't have been more obvious that the treatments had already taken a toll. He walked from the hospital with help from Micah. His climb into the truck showed his misery and his expression became more grim with each passing mile.

The silent suffering grew until George yelled out, "Pull over! I'm gonna be sick."

Without a word, Micah threaded his way to the shoulder of the highway. George struggled with the door for a second before shoving it open. Micah sat helpless as his father retched repeatedly. By the time the episode had ended, Micah was weak and shaking. But a glance at his father told Micah his suffering was nothing compared to how his dad felt right then. He passed a stack of napkins to his dad so he could clean up. The rest of the trip was a study in misery. George looked awful and he didn't say a word to Micah about how fast he was driving.

Micah had never been so relieved to turn into their driveway but the scene before them stunned him. There were a couple of vehicles parked around the house. He recognized one pickup as it's driver stepped from the barn with an armload of hay. *Lee.* And moving like his shadow, Kenny carried a bucket in each hand. Micah scowled as he came to a stop, but his own worries became pointless when he glanced at George and saw he was fighting to keep down whatever was left in his stomach.

Micah climbed out, raced to the other side and opened the door for his father. By that time, Lee and

Kenny had made their way to the pickup. Puzzled by their presence, he turned to Lee. "What are you guys doing? I've got everything covered."

Lee cocked an eyebrow. "The squeeze asked me to come help you."

Micah glanced first at Lee then to Kenny as he battled with conflicting emotions — elation that Tyler wanted to aid him and frustration that he might not see Micah as capable. He decided his life would be easier if he didn't argue when he had help. Then he realized these two weren't the only ones waiting. A figure rose from the shadow of the deep porch where they had an old-fashioned swing. They moved a few steps closer before Micah recognized who it was, but when he did, it shocked his system. It was Tyler's mother.

She gave Micah a short nod then turned to George. Micah found himself pushed to the periphery while Mary Lou talked with his dad in a low voice as they made their way toward the house. Micah watched until they disappeared into the dark entryway.

He noted Kenny was close enough to hear everything, and he turned to Lee. "What's going on? I can take care of my dad."

Lee appeared unrepentant. "The boss called and said that until I'm told otherwise, we're spending part of the day helping with the livestock."

"And George's garden," Kenny said.

Lee glanced at the youngster then nodded. "Yes...and the garden."

Micah glared at them then let out the breath he'd been holding before he continued. "And Mary Lou?"

Lee shrugged. "She arrived before we did and took over the porch swing." His smile grew even larger. "I figure it's only fair to warn you that I'm sure she brought enough groceries for a week."

"Oh, hell, no!" Micah said.

Lee laughed at the obvious scowl on Micah's face.

"Why did she do that? We had plenty of food in the fridge, what with Dad's precious vegetables and the beef from last year. There's no reason for her to bring groceries," Micah said.

Lee's eyebrows lifted higher. "You do realize Mary Lou is close to the same age as George, and Tyler's dad left her when he was a toddler."

"Oh, crap. No way! She can't be after dad."

Lee's laughter rang out and it was several minutes before he regained control enough to speak. "You keep telling yourself that, buddy."

Chapter Nine

A trickle of fear ran down the back of Tyler's neck. He'd arrived at the latest rodeo the previous night. On average, it was no different from any other town its size in the Southwest. The people were friendly and left each other alone. But the diner he'd had breakfast in was less relaxed than your typical rural eating establishment. Tyler wrote it off to a set of nerves from trying to keep up with everything going on at home.

It had been a few weeks since George had started the second round of treatments, but he still had more sessions left than anyone wanted to think about. Micah had stopped fighting against having help. Between everyone, they had worked out the details of when and how each person would fit in. It did little to alleviate his concern when his mother's reports were less hopeful than what Micah had told him. Any of these could contribute to his case of nerves but somehow, he didn't think that was it.

He'd went back to double-check his rig. He found Rusty agitated, which didn't make anything better. He spent the morning close to his nervous mount while he did a few maintenance items he'd been putting off for weeks. The bits of repair work he finished relaxed him. Nothing happened and some treats for the horse calmed Rusty.

After a few additional hours, he was happy to finish all the little chores he'd been avoiding. He also realized his stomach was growling. He agreed with it that lunch sounded like a good idea. After a few more snacks for Rusty, he ducked into the living quarters and got out the sandwich fixings. It didn't take long before Tyler had a plate piled high with food and a huge glass of whole milk sitting beside it. He flipped on the local television station and watched the news, but soon the latest weirdness on the national scene had his gut back in knots. He found all the drama disturbing and searched for programming that was not as life-threatening, but he still couldn't settle on a show so he turned off the TV.

He ate the rest of his meal with no sound but the whirr of the air conditioner in the ceiling and Rusty's occasional snorts. Once he'd put everything back in its proper place, he realized he was running low on some supplies, and if he didn't get what he needed, he'd be back in his college days of feasting on ramen. He entered the shopping list into his phone, and after one last paranoid triple-check, he headed to the local grocery.

He moved through the store, picking up items on his list. The uneasiness came back with a renewed strength. By the time he'd found the last item, his nerves were a twisted mess.

The young woman who checked him out kept glancing at him, making him more concerned with each passing second. She seemed as glad to see him leave as he was to exit the store.

Tyler was halfway across the parking lot when several men appeared. It didn't take a genius to realize this group was after him. *Why would I be their target?* He didn't understand, only that it was obvious these guys were out to hurt him.

The expressions on their faces were grim as they closed the distance between them and Tyler. He searched for a place where he would have something at his back and noticed a concrete wall that flanked one side of the parking lot. Tyler glanced around, saw they were moving closer and dropped into a dead run.

He reached the barrier a few steps ahead of the closest man. As he spun toward them, determined to make this a costly attack, he heard the sickening sound of a hunting blade snapping open. Cold chills ran down Tyler's spine but he fought against the sense of impending disaster. His heart dropped even further at the sight of a fourth person running toward Tyler and the group of thugs. To make the situation worse, the new attacker swung a bat in one hand. *A knife and a club. What a great combination.*

The knife-wielder skidded to a stop outside arms' reach, glaring at Tyler. Time slowed to a crawl while he stayed poised for the inevitable lunge. Just as he sensed the shift in position of his attacker, a shrill scream filled the air.

Confused, Tyler tried to work out what was happening and wondered if someone else had been too close and had been swept into the mess. But, after a glance, he realized there were fewer men running toward him. He didn't dare change his focus, but the farthest man was chasing down the one in front of him.

What the hell's going on?

In that moment of distraction, the attacker jumped forward with a slash of his blade. Tyler wasn't as lucky this time and the knife bit into his shoulder. The pain seared through his system, but he discovered that while the cut burned like hell, his arm still functioned. Then the scream of agony sounded again, but this time it was his attacker who glanced back in concern. A second later, a big blond man materialized from around a row of vehicles, screaming a war cry and brandishing what was one of the biggest baseball bats Tyler'd ever seen. The thug hesitated before throwing the knife at him, running to an almost-invisible opening in the wall and disappearing. Tyler stood in disbelief, staring at the last place he'd seen his would-be murderer before the man had disappeared. He was even more surprised when he turned to face the other thugs. They were nowhere to be found. He could only guess they'd helped each other escape. The alternative terrified Tyler, the one where other people were involved.

In the next instant, he realized his savior was standing beside him, using the bat to hold himself up while he gasped for air. He smiled but could only nod and wave. Tyler turned his attention to the shoulder cut to find the sleeve sliced and the injury still dripping blood.

His savior evaluated the wound. "I think you need stitches."

Tyler studied the cut closer but shook his head. "I'm not ready for an emergency room trip. I'll just tape it up."

"You sure? We can help you get everything taken care of and get you back to the competition."

The second unfamiliar voice startled Tyler, but when he spun to the person, a lot of what happened made more sense. "You checked my cinch when it had trouble at an Oklahoma rodeo. Dustin... Dustin Lewis." He turned to his bat-waving rescuer. "So, you must be his husband, Shane."

About that time, it dawned on Tyler that Dustin was carrying a toddler on one hip. He looked amused at Tyler's expression of disbelief. "This little guy is Austin. He's Shane's nephew and is here with his dad for tonight's rodeo. Sam fell asleep, so we brought the kid with us to get groceries." Dustin twisted his face into a scowl. "Of course, we had no idea we would get involved with a rescue."

The toddler peered at Tyler before hiding his face against Dustin. He rocked the child as he turned again toward Tyler. "That cut's nasty. You sure you don't want us to take you for some stitches?"

Tyler checked the wound once more before turning back to the pair. "Something has made me uneasy all day. I don't think I want to chance it."

Shane stepped closer, turned the arm first one direction then the other. Once he'd inspected it, he looked at Tyler. "It's not too deep. It just bled a lot. We've got a good first-aid kit in the RV. We can take care of it now then redo it so it won't tear during the bulldogging competition."

Tyler studied one of the men then the other before speaking. "I appreciate y'all saving my butt, but if you don't mind me asking... Why?"

Dustin appeared uncertain when he glanced at Shane then Tyler. "Why what? Why did we help you when you were being jumped by three big-ass guys?"

"Dustin..."

"Sorry. Big, stupid guys."

Tyler ducked his head until he no longer wanted to laugh at Dustin being schooled. It didn't take long before he could continue. "Yeah, I mean, anyone should help when someone is being jumped, but you two are the only ones who helped me of all the people who saw it happen. The others ran for their cars and left me to deal with those guys."

Austin was getting fussy and started the beginnings of a fit. Dustin sniffed in the general area of his butt. He turned to Shane and said, "Ah! It's your turn."

Tyler chuckled when Shane grimaced as he took the child. A second later, he held the little stink-bomb at arm's length. Dustin made shooing motions in Shane's direction. "It's your turn, dude. And make sure you leave the nuclear waste behind. That smell will peel paint."

Dustin turned back to Tyler. "Sorry. I got sidetracked. You asked me why we'd save someone I'd only met once before. I guess there are a lot of reasons, but mainly it's the decent thing to do, and if more people did something, then maybe this shit would stop."

"I heard you," Shane yelled from where he was changing Austin.

"Oh, shut up," Dustin called back then he turned again. He also spoke a little softer, causing Tyler to lean closer. "The second reason is more personal. Before we were married, Shane got attacked by a bunch of haters. They almost killed him and might have if me and my friend Todd hadn't jumped in and helped run them off. But because of that, neither of us would let something happen without trying to help."

There was a pause and Dustin grinned. "Besides, I know you. I wouldn't let another rodeo rider get attacked."

Tyler nodded in understanding. "Well, I appreciate you saving me but I can tape myself. I don't want to put you out any more than I have already."

Dustin snorted. "I ride bulls and the big guy lets them chase him. Wrapping each other is a fun Saturday night for us."

Shane stepped around the truck, cradling the baby in the crook of one arm. "Dustin's right. It won't take but a minute."

"Okay, all ready. I'd hate to waste all the good saving you did."

"Exactly."

During the next few minutes, Tyler's sense of foreboding built again. They couldn't leave soon enough. They'd strapped Austin in his seat and Dustin had climbed behind the wheel of Tyler's pickup. He leaned against the passenger window and wished they would move faster. As they drove to the exit, two officers climbed from a cop car—the local police. Tyler's chest constricted and his blood ran cold as the cops stood in place and watched the three of them leave.

"That was creepy as hell," Dustin said.

"Yeah, this town is like we were in *Deliverance*."

Dustin nodded in agreement. "I'm glad this is a one-night rodeo. We're leaving as soon as they announce the results. There is a bad vibe about everything here, like this place was built on an Indian burial ground and now the spirits are fucking with them."

Tyler wrapped his arms around himself and shook his head, but he refused to speculate any further. It wasn't long before they were in the RV parking lot along the back fence of the fairgrounds. The coach they stopped in front of made his living quarters look tiny.

They sat for a few seconds before Dustin turned toward him.

"We don't own it. It's from my sponsors. Last year, we were using this tiny trailer you had to crawl into and we slept on top of each other." He paused for an instant before winking at Tyler. "Not that it wasn't fun sometimes, too."

Heat washed over Tyler's face as Dustin's laughter filled the truck. But a few seconds later they were walking into Dustin's RV. He had given Tyler a handful of gauze to press against his injury and he resisted the urge to see how bloody the bandage was when they arrived. Dustin did a great job of keeping him focused. He escorted Tyler into the living area and motioned him to one of the overstuffed chairs.

He stopped arguing with the bull rider, in part because there was no way he would win against the energy powerhouse that was Dustin. But the other reason was more ominous. He felt drained and nauseous. Tyler hoped he hadn't lost enough blood to have that kind of effect, but he questioned his choice to refuse to go to the hospital. He'd drifted away when Dustin eased the bloody gauze from the injury.

He remained a little dazed until Dustin cleaned the wound. The sting of the antiseptic wash brought Tyler back quicker than smelling salts would have. He struggled to escape the chair. Dustin glanced up. "Hey, Shane, put Austin down and come help me."

Shane patted the toddler and rocked him as he made his way to the bedroom. A second later he was holding Tyler while Dustin cleaned the cut and coated it with antibiotic cream. He prodded at it before he dressed the injury. Once he tucked the tail under, he looked satisfied. "It wasn't bad, and I think the butterfly dressing will help keep it from scarring too much." Dustin studied Tyler's face. "How are you?"

"I'll be okay in a bit. The cut was more painful than I'd thought."

"That's what I figured. You are kind of green around the gills. Let me get you something." Without waiting for a reply, he moved to the fridge and filled a plate with food. Tyler glanced over to see Shane chuckling, his meaty arms folded.

He nodded toward Dustin. "Don't waste your energy. He's a force of nature once he gets started. Your life will be a lot easier if you go along with him. Besides, you don't seem like you feel too good."

Tyler shook his head, but when he stood, a wave of nausea flooded over him, forcing him back into the chair. He gave Shane a little grin. "Some rest and something to eat would help. But I have to make sure Rusty is okay and get ready for tonight."

"I'll check on your horse if you tell me where you're parked. And you'll need to come back and we'll tape you up so it won't cause you any trouble tonight. You might as well rest. Do you want to use Austin's bed or crash where you are?"

His reply was still a work in progress when the refrigerator door shut and Dustin smirked at him. He held a huge tumbler of ginger ale over ice and a plate containing a pile of saltine crackers along with several other items that would be more filling. Dustin handed Tyler the glass and platter then motioned toward the food.

"Start with the ginger ale and crackers and see how everything is once you've finished. The other stuff I got was more solid, but I'm not sure how well it would stay down on an upset tummy."

Tyler chuckled. "Upset tummy?"

"Okay. It's possible that taking care of Austin is wearing off on me."

Tyler refrained from any other comments while he took a drink that quenched his parched throat. He sat quietly until he was certain it wouldn't have an effect he would regret. From that point, Tyler became focused on filling his belly. Shane stayed out of the way while Dustin kept the tumbler filled. By the time he'd finished the last bits, he was much better. He was so sleepy, though, that his yawns threatened to unhinge his jaw. After a second attempt at speech was foiled by more yawns, Shane slipped a light blanket from storage, pushed Tyler to the couch and covered him.

"Sleep will do you a world of good. We'll make sure you don't miss anything," Dustin said.

Tyler was so tired that it took all his effort to understand what he was being told. The last thing he remembered was Dustin saying, "You think he'll be okay?"

* * * *

It amazed Tyler how much better he felt after sleeping most of the afternoon. Austin was the one to wake him with a few well-placed baby fingers exploring his face. While the first wet finger in his nose startled Tyler, a second later his brain functioned and he realized he had become a new toy. He eased his eyes open and made cooing noises at the toddler.

"Hey, big fella. Looks like you're up from your nap." Tyler reached over and ruffled the baby's shock of almost-white hair. The little one studied Tyler for a few seconds before bursting into giggles and prancing in place.

"He likes you. Most people don't get his happy dance."

Tyler sat up and stretched before nodding to Shane. "He's a cutie and is going to break some hearts."

Shane chuckled. "He already does that and gets away with murder. God help us all once he hits puberty. But I'm afraid he's already got Dustin and I wrapped around his little finger."

Tyler's smile grew as he played with Austin for a few minutes before looking at his watch. He coaxed a last bubbling giggle from the baby then turned to Shane.

"Thanks again for everything. I can't begin to tell you how much I appreciate you saving my" — he glanced to the toddler who was staring at them — "rear end. I'm sure I would have been toast."

"Just glad we were there to help. Sit here and let me take care of the cut while Dustin entertains the little guy," Shane said.

Tyler eased into the indicated seat and tried not to flinch as Shane exposed the injury and cleaned the angry red line. As he ran the alcohol-soaked pad over the exposed wound, Tyler couldn't keep from sucking in a breath between his teeth.

Shane paused and looked at him. "I could still take you to the hospital."

He waited for the pain to subside and waved Shane back to work. "Do it. I don't have time for all the hospital crap. Just do it."

"You want a bullet to bite on or something?" Dustin asked as he rocked Austin in his arms.

Tyler laughed then shook his head. "No, I'll make it." He nodded toward Shane. "Go ahead and wrap me up. Putting it off isn't going to help."

Shane picked up where he'd left off, and Tyler gritted his teeth to get him through the next few minutes. He'd suffered through much worse but was still relieved when Shane finished. He moved his arm, first tentatively then with more vigor. Once he put it through its paces, he took the shirt Shane handed him and slipped it on.

"It's in good shape. I shouldn't have any problems. I owe you one." Tyler glanced at the time again and started to leave. "It's close enough to our run that Everett will have his undies in a knot."

Shane chuckled and opened the door. As Tyler scrambled away, he heard Shane call out, "If you need anything, let us know."

Tyler waved back before breaking into a jog to the trailer. He soon had Rusty ready and he caught up with Everett. He held out a hand to stop the tirade he knew was coming. "I know I'm late, but I got jumped again."

Everett worked his face into a snarl. "Whatever."

"Here. Take a look." Tyler pulled his shirt to one side so Everett could see the wound.

While the truth had been enough to silence Everett, he still looked like he'd been eating green persimmons. His mood didn't improve when the best they garnered was a third-place finish. Once the rankings were announced, he left for the next competition.

In reality, Tyler had finished higher than he feared he would. He was thrilled to have finished in the money at all. But regardless of how he'd placed, he would be in the grandstands to cheer Dustin on when he rode. Tyler had never had a vendetta with the bull riders, but having his life saved by one and his bullfighter husband made it easy for him to want to support Dustin.

Tyler glanced over to discover Shane leaning against the fence as the current rider shot into the arena riding an animal that was trying to mimic a tornado made of muscle and sinew.

"Hey, Shane. How're you doing? I wanted to check on Dustin's ride." He grinned. "Seemed like a good opportunity to try out that whole being-supportive thing."

Shane chuckled as he slipped into the open spot next to Tyler. "We've never turned away a friend. I'm here to cheer him on, too."

They found seats in the stands to watch and wait for Dustin. The next rides went by in silence before a question bubbled up inside Tyler. "Why do they only have one clown? I'd think they need at least two."

Shane's mouth drew into a thin line. "With some of the bulls they're using, they need three people in the ring."

With a note of frustration from Shane, Tyler turned to face him. "Why don't they have more, then?"

"They said no one else was available."

Tyler considered his response, but Shane continued before he could speak. "Yeah, I pointed out that I was experienced and even offered to do it for free. They said no."

This time Tyler didn't need to find words. "Why?"

"Well, the nicest version was they couldn't hire someone married to a bull rider."

"Hmm, I hate to say it, but you would have a vested interest in Dustin winning."

"I know, and I might have bought the pile of crap."

"But?"

"I overheard the chairman of the rodeo commission talking about the fags and that he'd shut down the whole thing before he'd hire one of those people."

"What an ass," Tyler said.

"That's what I thought, too. My major concern is that Dustin would get injured because of their ignorance, but there's not much I can do but hope he won't."

A moan traveled through the bleachers and their focus became riveted to the unfolding scene. It was apparent the bull rider was in trouble. He'd tangled in his ropes and the single bullfighter wasn't enough to distract the bull and free the rider. The bull took off at a dead run along the arena edge, dragging the cowboy.

From his expression, it was obvious that Shane was ready to charge down the bleachers to come to the rider's aid. But the grounds filled, and it was too late for him to be of help. A few seconds—which seemed like minutes—passed before they separated the two. Once the bull left the arena, rescuers swarmed the injured man. A second later, the ambulance arrived and the EMT's hustled to the still figure.

Shane shook his head. "It's not good. They aren't moving him and the tech's being extra cautious. I haven't seen the cowboy move, either. The dumbasses. This is bad."

Several minutes passed and the tension of the crowd built. When they lifted the stretcher and the young man made a barely noticeable wave, it sent the audience erupting into a frenzy of applause, cheers and screams of delight. He'd always thought bull riders were the adrenaline junkies of the rodeo and most of them hung around with each other. But now that Tyler had friends in the sport, he understood the danger more clearly.

While his concern grew, he realized Shane was still talking to him.

"I refuse to let Dustin get hurt because of their stupidity. I'm going down to the arena so I can help if something happens," Shane said. His face twisted in determination, and a second later, Shane was running down the bleachers, taking two and three steps at a time. He disappeared from Tyler's view for a few seconds before he reappeared, standing at one of the fence sections.

Satisfied that Shane was in a good place to help if needed, Tyler narrowed his focus to the chutes as Dustin lowered himself to the animal's back. Tyler's heart pounded in his chest. With a sudden explosion of metal and beef, the bull entered the arena with a number of crow hops that had Dustin looking like a cowboy bobble-head doll. From there, the animal worked into a series of spins that made Tyler a little motion sick, thinking about how that must feel.

The ride continued for what seemed like forever. Each time the bull moved, the powder under him spun up like tiny dust devils. Tyler gripped the bench he sat on until his knuckles ached. As the tension built in mind-numbing proportions, Tyler's apprehension grew until he had a lump in his throat and a knot in his gut. When the eight-second timer screamed its expiration, Tyler's emotions drained away.

Dustin worked himself into a position to exit the widow maker. The bull uncoiled again and snapped his hooves out behind him. Dustin blended with the movements of the bull until he used the momentum to launch into the heated Texas air. To Tyler's relief, Dustin had none of the issues of the previous rider. His well-deserved bravado landed him feet-first with a maneuver that would have shown any acrobat how to do a flip when you had a ton of angry animal helping with the throw.

Tonight everything had aligned and the bull left with no more fuss than the neighbor's milk cow. Once Tyler spotted where his two new friends had exited, he left the stadium and made his way into the contestant's parking.

"Hey, guys. Hold up."

They turned back. "Hey, sorry about the whole disappearing thing. I was so happy Dustin didn't get hurt that I forgot everything else."

"No worries. I'm leaving."

"Headed to Arkansas?"

"No...Cody. My hazer is from up there and wanted to give it a run. But as soon as it's over, I've set up to take some lessons from a guy who has a great rep for taking bulldoggers to the next level."

Shane cringed. "Well, be careful in Cody."

"Bad?"

"Great rodeo. We ran into a few bad apples is all," Shane said.

Tyler sighed. "Is it never going to end?"

Chapter Ten

Tyler slowed through another hairpin curve in a road that appeared to be constructed to hold the world's collection of them. He eased to the side to read the directions again. GPS was useless out here in the backside of eastern Montana. His instructions resembled something more in line with Lewis and Clark rather than anything from the past hundred years. He was familiar with driving by landmarks but Central Oklahoma could at least reliably produce a decent cell phone signal.

He hoped the trainer he'd come to work with turned out to be as good as the rumors Tyler had heard about this guy since he'd started hitting the rodeo circuit, but he'd never actually seen the man. It had taken him weeks to get the phone number for the elusive teacher then a few more days of obsessive calling before someone answered. Still, it had taken quite a bit of cajoling before he'd gotten the man's agreement and the oh-so-precious directions that were Tyler's current bane.

His previous directions were to have been indicated by an old schoolhouse beside it. There had been no doubt that the turn he'd taken had been marked by an ancient structure of some kind. Tyler hoped it had been an old schoolhouse. Anything he'd gone past for the last hundred miles must have been built in the previous century. But when he checked his odometer with the distance he needed to drive, it appeared he should be in the right vicinity.

Rusty shifted in the trailer and squealed. "Hang in there, buddy. Hopefully, we're close. Otherwise, we'll get you out and do a little lunge line." The sound of another stomp or two drifted to Tyler, but the horse seemed to understand.

He glanced at his well-worn paper and sighed. His final landmark? According to what he'd been given, he'd recognize it on sight. He crept into a canyon with a low-water crossing. He drove through the inches deep water and studied the area. The tiny stream made a world of difference for the high plains region dominated by buffalo grass for miles in any direction. A willow thicket crowded the pool below the crossing. In the distance, he was certain he saw evidence of beavers and other wildlife. The brief vignette gave Tyler more of the sense of peace he'd been missing. As he crawled up the steep, rural road, a flash of color caught his eye. Tied to the first mailbox he'd seen in several miles was a bright pink balloon.

Okay, the directions are right. I found the signal for the driveway entrance.

Tyler made the wide turn needed to get his rig onto the two-track trail headed away from the road. This time he got his confirmation about the destination without driving another interminable distance. He topped the ridge in front of him and he couldn't miss the tidy white home sheltered in the small valley, surrounded with a sprinkling of outbuildings. He closed the distance then slipped the trailer under one of the large trees close to the house.

As he parked, Tyler noticed a figure seated on the porch and he waved. After getting an acknowledgment, he walked back to check on Rusty. The animal stuck its nose against Tyler's hand and blew out a hot breath. "Hang on. We'll have you out of there in short order."

"Put him in the big corral. He needs out of the trailer."

Tyler jumped to hear the deep rumbling voice beside him. He turned to find an elderly man in a cowboy hat and boots keeping an eye on him. He recovered and offered his hand. "Hi, you must be Mr. Old Crow. I'm Tyler. Thanks for agreeing to work with me."

When the man didn't answer, Tyler realized he was being tested, but he tolerated this kind of thing with no problem.

After a short time, while ignoring the offered hand, the man spoke. "*Kahée*. Carl's fine to call me. I don't hold much on formality. Take the horse to the corral so he can stretch out. While he's relaxing, you can set up your trailer by the barn. Lunch is almost ready, so once you get him settled in, come to the house." With that, he turned and left Tyler standing with his mouth open.

Tyler stared after him but realized he'd gotten marching orders. He led Rusty to the pen Carl had indicated. The horse acted thrilled to have room to run and soon he raced around the enclosure with his tail held high. Tyler watched for a few minutes before filling the manger with alfalfa, one of the animal's favorites. When Rusty seemed settled into the new surroundings, Tyler headed toward the house. *This guy is supposed to be the Yoda of steer wrestling but I hope he isn't just another over-hyped old-timer. Rodeo brings out the freaky superstitions more than other sports.* He hoped Carl would give him pointers that would get him back into a winning focus.

He knocked on the door in spite of being told it wasn't necessary. It somehow seemed disrespectful to walk into the home of someone he'd just met. But a few seconds later he heard, "It's open. I'm in the kitchen getting food on the table."

This time Tyler didn't hesitate. As he walked through the living room, he noticed the mass of rodeo photographs that covered the walls. He wanted to look at them more carefully, but his mother had taught him what it meant when the cook said the food was going on the table, and it wasn't a time to gawk at photos.

He stepped a little faster and entered a bright room with two walls of windows and a cool breeze winding its way between them. Carl nodded to an empty chair as he sat a huge Dutch oven in the center of the table. He brought two glasses of ice water and put one in front of Tyler. Carl slid into his seat without a word and filled his bowl from the cooking pot. Once he'd finished, he turned the ladle to Tyler, who dished up a helping of the heavenly smelling meal.

Carl focused on him and seemed to have no issues studying him openly. Tyler lifted a spoonful and blew on it. Once the steam stopped rising from the food, he slipped it into his mouth. He chewed cautiously but enjoyed the flavor. As he swallowed the tidbit, Carl said, "Elk."

Tyler blinked and tried to process the statement. But Carl explained before the question left Tyler's lips. "The chili... It's made from elk — one my cousin got last fall. I think it tastes better than beef, but I thought I'd tell you, in case it tasted off to you."

Tyler shook his head, a little overwhelmed with the sudden blurt of information and he wondered if it indicated how their working relationship might progress. "No, I think it's delicious. A friend of mine is an avid hunter and makes a mean pot of venison chili. This tastes even better."

Carl nodded. "It's the elk."

Contrary to Tyler's hopes, the exchange marked the end of their mealtime conversation. He hoped the situation would become more tolerable with time. *I'm trusting this trip isn't a huge mistake, but I need something to give me a kick in the butt.* All these second and third place finishes would not get him into the National Finals.

Carl stood and put away the food before slipping the dishes into the sink. At some undetermined point, Carl must have decided everything was in a passable order and he turned to Tyler.

"Your horse should be rested. Ready for me to check your technique?"

Caught off-balance, he stared at Carl for a second or two then shot up, slid his chair under the table and turned to Carl. "Sure thing. I'm ready to make a run at it."

Carl nodded and motioned Tyler to an exit through the mud room then outside. Tyler had to move fast to keep up. When they reached the pen, he stopped to watch Rusty for a few seconds. "You took care of your horse first. That's good."

Tyler found himself startled enough that his next words were unfiltered. "Anyone who doesn't take care of their animal first is an idiot. You win or lose because of your horse."

Carl cocked his brows but broadened his smile. "I have a lot of idiots through here, then." He turned back to the horse, who was swishing its tail. "Let's see how you work together."

Tyler turned to retrieve the saddle but Carl stopped him. "You don't need that. I want you to go through a few runs without any junk getting in the way."

A quiver of doubt writhed through Tyler but he didn't comment. Then another thought occurred to him. "Can I use the bridle?"

Tyler would have sworn he caught a twinkle in Carl's eye. "I think using a hackamore would be fine. We don't want one of you to get injured the first day."

Tyler fetched the headgear for the horse that he needed and walked into the pen with Rusty. With one of the horse's favorite treat in one pocket, he had no difficulty catching and bridling his mount. As they moved out, Tyler got the hopeful impression that their performance so far had pleased Carl.

They moved a few hundred feet behind the house to one of the working arenas. It was obvious from its construction that the only event it hosted was bulldogging. When they reached the gate, Tyler stopped and waited for more instruction.

Tyler detected another glimmer of approval before Carl explained his goal for this exercise. "I want you to work on controlling your horse with only your legs."

Tyler considered the directive and had no difficulty seeing the logic. He and Rusty already had experience along those lines and Tyler didn't think they would have problems.

He was so wrong.

Their first try was fine for the initial steps, then Rusty moved to a gallop—one Tyler felt he had no control over. Within a few seconds, he was grabbing for the reins and thanking the gods that Carl had agreed to let him use the bridle.

The next handful of attempts met with failure. They ranged in disaster level from bad to near train wreck. Tyler's concentration had left him shaking from the effort. *It's obvious I don't understand this horse as well as I thought.* Rusty appeared unfazed by the experience, but sweat had soaked Tyler's shirt by the time Carl stopped the exercise.

"About what I expected. You should be working toward the same goal. Right now, he's not clear what you want. Walk him around the arena and try to not use the reins."

By the end of the session, Rusty showed signs of frustration and Tyler thought this trip was a waste of time and money. He wished Micah were with him so he had another, less exhausted, viewpoint on this whole thing, but he had been the one who had begged Carl to work with him for a week. He wouldn't quit and retreat south after a single frustrating day.

"Try again."

Tyler studied the man then shook his head. "Rusty acted up after that last try. He needs a break."

Carl watched the horse fidget in place, walked over and opened the gate for them. He motioned toward a nearby building. "Stable's in there. There are several empty stalls. Pick whichever he'd be the most comfortable in. There's a shower in the bathroom. Once you're cleaned up, come to the house and I'll have supper ready." Without another word, he left.

Tyler stared at the older man as he walked around the corner. *Good Lord, what have I gotten myself into?*

The first day set up a working relationship for the next. The instructions were obscure and Tyler decided at one point that Carl was working to make him feel stupid, and there were fewer things in life that Tyler hated more than being trivialized. The next day evolved into a battle of wills and Tyler knew he wasn't going to win. Carl set him back on the task from the first day. With a single stop for lunch, Tyler spent his day trying to control his horse using some kind of Jedi mind junk that was actually made up to make him crazy. By the time he was having supper, he was too exhausted to do more than eat before collapsing into the bed.

On the third day working with Carl, Tyler wasn't able to tell that the relationship between him and his horse had changed much. Not that the two of them'd had a bad relationship before. but Carl appeared to want them to have an almost telepathic connection. Fortunately, Tyler's attitude had improved. There was a simple enough reason for that. The previous night he'd had a long conversation with Micah. The status updates on George left him concerned, but Micah had explained the treatment was going the way the doctor hoped. He'd also given Tyler the buck-it-up-buckaroo speech and had him chuckling. But Micah had pointed out that only a few days remained, and he might have already learned more than he thought.

He led Rusty from the stables to find Carl standing with one of his horses bridled. "You know about different groups being skilled horseback archers? That's how the people of the plains hunted buffalo."

He nodded, a little concerned about what new idea Carl had concocted. Then he realized Carl had brought a recurve bow out with him.

"Good. I've decided you need a focus. Otherwise, the horse doesn't know where to go because you don't give him a clear message." Carl swung onto his mount with the grace of someone who had been working with horses their entire life. He motioned toward a flat area a short distance away.

"I set up a course through there and scattered a few 3-D archery targets through it," Carl said. He turned to Tyler with a smirk. "I don't expect you to hit anything. The bow takes time to master. But the trying is what I want. I'll show you."

Carl fastened a quiver of arrows across his back and nocked the first arrow to the bowstring. They arrived at the beginning point and Tyler moved to one side so he wouldn't be in the way. Carl's concentration snapped into place as he leaned forward and the horse lunged toward the targets.

His mentor rode the circuit, and it amazed him. Now he understood how the legend of the centaur came into being—with ancient horsemen at Carl's skill level. A second later, he released the shaft, and it appeared quivering in the kill zone of the mule-deer target. A handful of arrows flew from his bow with equal accuracy.

Tyler worked to implement the riding style Carl had been trying to teach him all week. He considered the fine details of the ride he hadn't been able to understand from an explanation. The dance of shifting balance points and tightening muscles moved Carl in ways that reminded him of Dustin's winning ride on the bull. As Carl rose for the final target, the horse shifted to compensate.

Tyler stood in awe as Carl trotted back to him. "That was amazing!" Tyler said.

Carl leaned down and patted the horse's neck. "We've been together for a long time. That makes a great deal of difference." He slipped off the arrows and handed them to Tyler, along with the bow. "Do what you can. We'll make adjustments after the first run."

Tyler attached the quiver so he could pluck arrows from it as he moved through the course. After doing a mental check, he shifted his weight forward and Rusty leaped down the path.

Carl had been correct. By focusing on the targets, he gave the horse all the guidance needed. He snatched an arrow from the carrier, drew back to his cheek and released. Tyler had an instant to revel at the sight of the shaft vibrating in the foam target as they galloped past. His heart pounded in his chest as they bore down on the trio of targets ahead of them. He released three shafts in rapid succession to equal triumph. For the rest of the course, Tyler and his mount worked in perfect unison and shot with deadly accuracy. By the time he released the final arrow, his body had filled with the adrenaline overload of a successful hunt. He spun and raced to Carl, thrusting both hands in the air. At the last second, he slid to a stop and shook from a system flooded with excitement.

"I got it! It worked right. That was amazing."

Carl lifted a brow but the expression on his face reflected Tyler's joy at success. "Nice. Good shooting, too. I don't think you missed any of them."

"It felt right. I see how it would work with the steers, too."

"Good. Then gather up the arrows and we'll go through it again."

By late afternoon when Carl stopped them for the day, Tyler barely had the capability to string together two words and he had improved little by the time he sat across from Carl at the dinner table. He sliced into the piece of elk roast and gathered mashed potatoes, too exhausted to have even their usual minimal exchange. He snapped himself back to the present when Carl cleared his throat.

"Did you get through to your friend last night?" Carl asked.

Tyler considered his reply for a few seconds. He knew the evening might go in several directions. This could be the end of their unusual friendship. "Yes, I got to check on everything."

Carl nodded and returned to the meal. Tyler let some time pass, but soon the weight of having left Carl with a misconception became disturbing. He'd had worked his entire life at being satisfied with himself. He considered then shook his head. "Micah and I are dating."

"You're with another man?"

Tyler's stomach roiled into a knot, but he'd already started this conversation. "I'm gone a lot, but we try to share our time whenever we can. His father is in chemotherapy, so I try to touch base as often as possible."

Carl met his gaze with a considered expression then continued eating with no further questions. Tyler tried to let it go until the tension wore on him. "Is that going to be an issue? I can leave if you'd like."

Carl stopped with a full fork halfway to his lips and locked eyes with Tyler. "That you're *badé*?"

Now, it was Tyler's turn to be confused. "What's *badé*?"

Carl took the bite of food and chewed it while he continued to study Tyler. Once he'd swallowed, he explained. "Most of your world view is from a white standpoint. Did you know that most of the tribes recognized three to five genders? It's too easy to say when I use the term *badé* that it translates from Crow to English as gay, because there is a lot more to it. But no, I don't care, and I'll leave it to your culture to solve the problems they have caused over their interpretation."

A smile formed across Tyler's face and the python that had been coiled through his stomach released its hold. "I like your way of thinking."

Carl waved his fork in the air and shot Tyler a mischievous expression. "That's because we're right."

Tyler chuckled and returned to the food, which tasted better than anything he'd eaten in a long time.

With the breakthrough in the training, the next few days flashed past. On his final morning, he was a little surprised when Carl knocked at his door.

"Let's go. The steers are coming." Carl turned and headed toward the arena.

Tyler took a few hops to get his boot on, grabbed his cowboy hat and raced after Carl. Once he'd caught up, Tyler walked a few steps to catch his breath before asking anything. "What steers? You don't have any steers."

"Nope," Carl said as he motioned to the road running through the crest in the ridge, "but my nephew does."

A few seconds later, Tyler's jaw dropped when a gooseneck trailer full of bellowing cattle topped the hill. Before Tyler could gather his thoughts, they'd backed up to the gate. He took off to help the two people who'd delivered the animals unload. Once they'd finished, Carl turned to him. "Unless you're going to run them down on foot, you're going to need that horse of yours." Tyler sprinted toward the stables to retrieve Rusty. With the practice of years of repetition, he was in the arena in a few minutes. He'd positioned himself in the starting box before he glanced up to find a young woman ready to haze for him. Again, not at his best for explanations, he stammered out, "Carl said his nephew was bringing the steers."

She laughed at him. "Dad is Carl's nephew, so I guess that makes me a great-niece. But most of the folks around here call him Uncle. And, by the way, I'm Gracie."

Carl glanced at the two of them. "You two finished with the introductions?"

Tyler looked away but Gracie grinned wider. Both of them moved the horses until they were in perfect position and he gave a quick nod. With the exchange, the world exploded around Tyler and he entered what he'd come to think of as buffalo hunt mode where he used the skills needed for hunting buffalo while on a horse bulldogging. Rusty flowed under him like never before and they flanked the steer. With a twist of his body, he launched toward the animal, and a second later, its four legs were in the air. Carl waved him in. "Put on your saddle. It's time to put what you've learned into action."

He gave a quick nod before charging through the gate and to the trailer where he saddled Rusty. When he returned, it impressed him how calm everyone was, but then the others didn't have their careers hinging on the next few rides. They readied everything and a second animal leaped out of the chute.

To use the saddle for the first time in a week left Tyler with a sense of disconnect. The leather felt like another obstacle. But he put his issues aside and started his descent—and the cinch snapped. Tyler disregarded the saddle and focused on his prey. The takedown was as flawless as he might have asked when the steer flipped onto its back. By the time Tyler was on his feet, Gracie had caught Rusty and they were only a few yards from Tyler.

"What happened? Did the strap break?" Gracie asked.

Tyler frowned. "I think so. I've had problems with the cinch all summer."

Carl picked up the strap and studied it before turning to Tyler. "It isn't a knife cut, but something weakened the leather. You need to keep an eye on these issues or you'll get hurt. For today, I want you to use one of my saddles. I'm sure I have one that will work."

Tyler made the change, but the question of the reliability of his equipment loomed over him with the sense of impending disaster. But Tyler realized riding saddled came easier and Gracie was as good a hazer as Everett, although that piece of information he planned to keep close to his chest.

With the successful ride under his belt and a safe saddle on Rusty, they focused on duplicating the first run. The repetition settled him into the actual chase. It didn't take long to discover that Gracie wasn't Everett's equal. She was, by far, his superior. During one of their breaks in the afternoon, his curiosity overcame him.

"You're a fantastic hazer. Why haven't you teamed up with someone and hit the circuit?"

She studied Tyler over the lip of the ladle that had been in the bucket of crystal clear water. Her dark eyes twinkled as she put the dipper back on the nail it hung from. "I'm happy here. I like to travel, but I want to come home at the end of the trip. My family are all in this part of Montana. I can't imagine living anywhere else and I would miss my people."

As she finished, Carl joined them and got himself a drink. Tyler began to think he hadn't heard their exchange but then he shifted his eyes to Tyler. "Family gets to be more important as you get older. I'm an old man, so I need relatives helping me all the time."

Gracie snorted and Tyler glanced at her in time to see them exchange glances. *I think there is some inside joke I don't know.* Then the focus shifted back.

"Okay. Enough time counting prairie dogs. Let's run them again."

Tyler exchanged puzzled looks with Gracie. She shrugged. "Don't ask me. One of Uncle's cockeyed sayings." But after the humorous exchange, the day soon exhausted itself.

The rest of the daylight hours wound to an end, Tyler's skill improved and he found himself sad to be leaving. The work had been grueling, but he'd learned more than just the fine points of bulldogging. He closed the trailer gate and turned to find Carl at his side.

"You did better than anyone has in years. You listened to the old guy. It's been a long time since I've enjoyed a student as much as you."

Tyler said, "I wasn't too sure I would make it through those first few days."

Carl smirked. "They had a purpose, and you did well with them. You surprised me with your archery skills." A pause grew as he became more somber. "The saddle strap concerns me. It's dangerous, and I see no reason for it to happen."

A sense of loss washed over Tyler and his gaze darted like a dragonfly from one thing to another, wanting strong memories of this place where he had changed so much. As the desperation reached an unreasonable level, a hand came to rest on his shoulder and squeezed. He turned to find Carl wearing an expression of sympathy.

"You are welcome here," Carl said. A second later he continued with a smile. "You will always be able to find the last turn."

A weight lifted from Tyler, and on impulse, he again extended his hand to Carl. This time, instead of the invitation being ignored, he got a firm handshake. Tyler fought back tears as he traveled over the ridge, but as the ranch slipped behind the horizon, Carl stood in front with his hand extended toward the sky.

With a snap that bordered on audible, Tyler re-entered his world.

Chapter Eleven

A wide smile was plastered across Micah's face as he watched Tyler come up their driveway. Tyler's schedule had been such that it had been several weeks since he'd been able to visit, so they'd had nothing more than text messages, phone calls and the occasional video chat. But a few days earlier, Tyler had told him he would be home by the end of the week. Micah knew it would be a short break from the circuit, but he would take what Tyler gave him. The sight of the familiar truck wheeling down the road had Micah's pulse racing with excitement. The wait had been too long and Micah wanted to hold Tyler in his arms.

Almost before the pickup came to a complete stop, Tyler bailed out and bolted toward Micah, who sprinted to Tyler. They wrapped their arms around each other and shared a passionate embrace. Micah held on tight, wrapping his legs around Tyler as they pressed their lips together. The heat of their passion for each other left Micah aching for Tyler's touch. His desire for Tyler had him driven to the point where he would have done Tyler on their porch. Fortunately, reality overrode the heat of passion and common sense prevailed.

Micah peeled himself off but couldn't do more than stand with his hands on Tyler's shoulders and grin.

"I'm so glad to see you. How are things?" Micah asked.

"I spent a week with the bulldogger whisperer I told you about. That was kind of cool."

"Did it help?"

Tyler thought about the question. "Yeah, it did. His methods are a little out of the normal, but I've won the last three rodeos. At the one a few days ago, no one else was even close. But enough about rodeo, I'm so damn glad to see you."

"George is asleep but I'm not. You two need a room."

Micah turned to find Kenny standing behind the screened door, watching. "Go read the horticulture magazines, Kenny. We'll be inside in a few minutes." He turned and whispered to Tyler. "Kenny came out to go with Dad to the master gardening classes. Once they got home, Dad went to take a nap and Kenny spread the class materials out on the table so he could study them."

Micah gave Tyler another peck on the cheek before they separated and turned to the house. As they made their way into the living room, Kenny glanced at them and Micah saw the smirk on his face.

Micah settled on one end of the couch and squirmed into a comfortable position as Tyler followed his example and sat in the overstuffed chair. Micah considered where to begin, and he decided his best option was to ask about the bulldogger lessons, since they'd had the biggest impact on Tyler. He knew he'd hit the motherlode when Tyler started detailing all the things that had happened to him in a breathless flurry. The recounting of Tyler's adventures became more interesting as each part of the story unfolded.

By the time Tyler had revealed the last day's events, Micah knew he wanted to meet Carl at some point.

"So, he's a member of the Crow tribe?" Micah asked.

Tyler considered the question before shrugging. "I figure he is. He used a few words that weren't English, but he never said. I didn't ask. It seemed impolite, and if Carl needed me to know something, he wasn't shy about telling me."

"I could see that. It sounds like it was an amazing experience."

"It was. The trip of a lifetime."

They lost themselves catching up on the events since the last time they had been together. Micah enjoyed the time and soon their typical relaxed conversation returned. Tyler was recounting one of his recent winning rides when noise erupted from the kitchen that sounded like every pan in the house had landed in the middle of the floor. He turned to Micah and lifted an eyebrow. "Are the elves on strike or something?"

"Kind of. Your mother and Kenny have Dad on a diet to fit his blood type. I didn't see any harm in it." He considered Tyler. "Mary Lou insisted on paying for everything, so it was a win-win situation in my book."

"Is it helping?"

"It's hard to tell but he doesn't get sick as often. Kenny has him on a strict low-carb regimen, which might be part of it."

"Kenny's cooking for your dad?"

Micah chuckled. "Yeah, down to a bedtime snack. Dad has a dorm fridge in his room now, so the snacks are right there whenever he wants them."

Tyler stared toward the kitchen for a short time before turning back to Micah. "How did the kid get so involved? His community service thing I worked out with his mother ended weeks ago. I thought he'd be long gone."

"No, not only did he not quit but he's here more. His mom drops him off early Saturday and Sunday, and during the week, he rides the school bus out here. It's thrilling his mother."

"And he's doing it all for free?"

Micah said, "I think Lee's slipping him some cash every Friday."

"That sounds like Lee." Tyler made a slight frown before continuing, "but I should talk to Mom about putting Kenny on payroll. Lee has enough kids without taking on another responsibility."

Micah started to argue with him about spending money on Kenny when he was helping at their ranch, not where Tyler had hired him to work, but when he glanced at Tyler, the bulldogger grinned at Micah with one eyebrow lifted. He decided that arguing with Tyler about paying Kenny might be the right thing to do but that it wasn't a great time to climb on that soapbox.

He gave Tyler a theatrical scowl. "Don't assume you won. I'm just too tired to put out the effort to argue."

Tyler chuckled, grabbed Micah by the back of the neck and leaned close. "What do you think about a little — "

"Dinner's ready!"

Micah glanced toward the kitchen — and Kenny — before turning back to Tyler. "Did I mention everything is on a schedule?" Micah chuckled as they made their way to the dinner table. He had to admit it all smelled delicious. And after eating these meals for several days, he enjoyed the food. When he looked at Tyler, he could tell the bulldogger had his doubts about the change, doubts that pretty much matched Micah's initial response.

Tyler used his fork to lift the edge of a green pancake that was on his plate. When he tilted his head, looked at Micah and lifted his eyebrows until they almost met his hairline. It took all of Micah's effort to keep from laughing. Tyler's expression was as close to disgusted as he'd ever seen. It was a full blown 'spoon full of cod-liver oil' expression.

Micah sensed a need to help Tyler in what was becoming a strained moment.

"The green pancake things are kale and kimchee — "

"And it's all supposed to cure me, according to Mary Lou and her voodoo people," Dad said as he shuffled through the doorway. He caught Tyler's expression and shook his head. "It's not that bad. Kenny's good at making it, so everything is tasty and piping hot, but it won't be for much longer if we're standing here jawing."

Taking his dad's comment to heart, Micah passed the trays of food. The small group had settled into the meal when the dogs exploded from their usual spots and raced to the front door, barking ferociously. Micah followed them there in time to spot the sheriff's car come to a stop among the other vehicles. Micah glanced back to the gathering at the table, "It's a car from the sheriff's office. Have you been busted for moonshining again, Dad?"

"That wasn't moonshine. It was homemade wine—
and far below the limit for hobby production. Now, if
you're not too busy being disrespectful to your father,
we can go see what's wrong."

Micah chuckled at the idea of anyone getting away
with being flippant to his father. He knew that would
be a bad choice, so he kept his views to himself and
walked toward the police car. Once they were a little
closer, he saw the deputy was Jackson, a friend from
high school.

Micah took the offered hand and gave him a firm
shake. "Hey, Jack. What brings you out to the sticks?"

He nodded to everyone as Tyler joined the first two.
Micah noted that Kenny was nowhere in sight, but he
knew the kid would be watching from somewhere.
Once he'd greeted each of them, the officer began his
explanation. "The sheriff has us warning people that
we've had some drifters around for a few days. They
are stirring up a little crap, just grown men acting like
testosterone-filled kids. They're also good at avoiding
local law enforcement, so we haven't had our friendly
chat with them yet."

"Anything we should be concerned over?" Micah
asked.

"Nothing specific, but they're spoiling for trouble. It's
as if they're hunting for someone." There was a
moment's hesitation before Jackson went on. "Actually,
they're asking around and the description they're
giving sounds like y'all, so I thought I'd stop by and tell
you to keep an eye out for a strange truck. Have you
had any problems?"

"No," Micah said.

There was a pause before Tyler answered, "Yeah, we
have had incidents on the circuit. It's starting to feel a

little stalkerish, like we'd pissed off some backwoods family."

Jack nodded. "That would fit what we've learned. If there are problems, let us know."

They chatted for a few more minutes before exchanging goodbyes, and the police car was soon disappearing into the distance. With everyone wrapped in their own thoughts, Kenny reappeared and looked like he expected to be told why the cops had been at the ranch. At least, that was what his expression said. With everyone wrapped in their own thoughts, they made their way back to the table. The tension built as the silence stretched out until the false peace ended and everything came crashing back to them.

"We need to check the rifles, clean our pistols and start wearing them again," George said.

Before he went further in his tirade, Micah shook his head. "Dad, I'm sorry but I disagree. I refuse to arm myself because someone has become threatening. I'm more worried that some innocent bystander would get hurt."

Micah could sense the tension rolling over them when Tyler cleared his throat. When they looked toward him, he nodded in Kenny's direction. At the reminder, the fight drained from Micah and George went pale.

"Sorry, Dad. We can talk about the guns later."

He patted Micah on the shoulder. "That's fine. Let's finish dinner. I hear there's dessert tonight."

The rest of the meal was subdued, but it made Micah happy that the tension had dissipated. Once dinner had ended, he and Tyler helped clean the kitchen. Once everything was in its place, Micah found his father asleep in the recliner as one of the television shows he enjoyed flickered across the screen. He woke George so he could tell him where they were going.

"Tyler and I are headed to the bar for some R&R. We'll drop Kenny off at his home when we go through town. I'll be back in a couple of hours. Don't worry. In the morning, we can decide what we're doing about the drifters."

George nodded. "Tomorrow. Your word on it."

"Yes, Dad. I promise we'll discuss it tomorrow, first thing. Get rested and enjoy your shows."

* * * *

Micah and Tyler found themselves at the local watering hole trying to relax, but the deputy's caution had Micah on edge. Every time the door opened, Micah glanced over to see who came through. After he'd repeated the reaction several times, Tyler leaned across their table.

"Jack's warning still wearing on you?" Tyler asked.

Micah sighed and nodded his head. "It is. Sorry to have screwed up our first evening together in a while."

Tyler checked his watch. "We told George you wouldn't be too late. Why don't we go back? You can make sure your dad is okay then we can relax with some TV."

Micah twisted his lips at the suggestion. "No fun for us."

Tyler's eyes twinkled as he finished his glass of beer. He got up from the table and motioned Micah ahead of him. "You'll live without making out tonight. You'll feel better if you know everything at the ranch is fine."

Micah led the way to the pickup and had no problem being the passenger for the trip home. He couldn't rid himself from the uneasy feeling but he kept his peace until they reached the front gate. His tension tripled in intensity and he grabbed Tyler's arm.

"Stop the pickup. Turn off the headlights. Something isn't right."

"You sure it's not just nerves?"

Micah hesitated for a few seconds, trying to decide why he had the feelings he did. Then it came to him.

"No, the dogs. They should be outside and raising hell at your truck being in the driveway but there's nothing."

Tyler remained still for a few seconds before he nodded in agreement. With his voice barely audible, he leaned close to Micah. "Got it. Any suggestions."

Micah studied their surroundings before beginning. "There're no lights. The power must be off. But we have to be careful. I don't want to make it worse for Dad. They've parked somewhere out of sight. You want to go around back? I'll see if I can't get through the kitchen. I don't know for certain where they are, but I'm guessing it's the living room," Micah said.

Tyler nodded and turned off the dome light so it wouldn't give them away when they opened the doors. Micah considered what he could use as a weapon but couldn't come up with anything. He decided time was not on their side and motioned for Tyler to start toward the house. They kept low as they worked their way across the gravel parking area and through the gate without making a sound. Once they were inside the yard, Tyler peeled away, heading for the back door.

A few steps farther and Micah found the evidence of one of his fears when he came upon Pepper's limp form on the other side of the sidewalk. Micah lifted the dog in a tight embrace as he allowed himself a few seconds to mourn his companion. As he eased the dog back to the ground, his anger and fear built.

He moved closer, doubling his caution. A short distance away, he found the other half of his pair of childhood companions. This time it wasn't a fatal injury. A soft whimper drifted to Micah, and a second later, he spotted Salt dragging herself to him with a series of whines accompanying each inch gained.

Micah abandoned stealth and shot to his suffering dog. She melted against the ground as he eased his hands over her, trying to find the injury. When he touched her hind leg, he got a yelp in response. After his hand came back wet and the air filled with the smell of blood, he feared she was bleeding out, even as he held her. He was terrified about his father, but still, he had to help his dog. He ripped off his shirt and fastened it as tight as possible around Salt's wound before heading toward the house. Then gunfire erupted in the quiet night, followed by voices he didn't recognize.

Afraid they had discovered Tyler, he covered the remaining distance in a sprint. He opened the door and dashed behind the kitchen cabinets. He readied himself for an assault on the living room when the lights flooded the house and a voice announced. "Come on, pretty boy, unless you want us to take care of your daddy and boyfriend like we did those damn dogs."

Micah glanced around, searching for a way to end this without injuries. He decided the best thing he could do was stall and hope the ones holding his dad and Tyler would do something wrong, but his dread built to new levels. He searched for a weapon and caught the glimmer of a blade left on the cutting board—a huge chef's knife, almost as long as his forearm. He slipped his hand up and worked to ease it off the edge. Micah hoped he'd managed it in a way that had hid his actions. He almost dropped it when his father spoke. "My son's not here. He high-tailed it to find the cops."

While his father drew their attention, Micah snatched the knife off the board and crouched against the cabinet as he tried to calm his racing heart. The weapon in his hand did little to accomplish his goal. These men had guns and had already used them to deadly effect. Then he heard Tyler speak. "George is right. I was supposed to stay away until he got the cops. Stupid me. I thought I could rescue George alone."

The crack of a skull being hit filled the room and Micah went weak at the knees. He didn't have much time and didn't know if he could get in a throw, but he had to locate where everyone was so he didn't hit George or Tyler. He belly-crawled across the kitchen tile to where he could peer into the living room. The sight before him was chilling. The men who had attacked them several months back were standing with guns trained on his father and Tyler. *They sure must hate us to have gone to such great lengths for this.* He didn't see how the situation could go any way but bad.

Then, as he studied the scene, he realized George sat at an odd angle in the chair they were holding him in. He shifted again and glimpsed pink in his dad's hand.

Shit! He has that damn little gun that only holds one bullet.

Micah didn't have time to do more as George yanked out the gun and shot the man holding him. Micah jumped to his feet and threw the kitchen knife with all the force he could muster. An instant later, the blade had embedded half its length in another of the attackers and the man fell to the floor, screaming.

Micah ducked behind the cabinet as soon as he launched the weapon and was happy he had when two quick rounds punched holes in the wall where he'd been standing.

"You're all gonna die!"

The gun that fired next wasn't anything small enough to hide in a robe pocket. He couldn't bear to see what had happened. He knew his father had sacrificed himself to save him and Tyler. But now...

"What the hell? I warn you to watch for some dangerous SOBs and you draw them in for a shoot-out? I ain't telling you a damn thing from now on."

Micah froze. *Jackson?*

He moved to one knee then stood as he surveyed the scene of the devastation. He breathed a sigh of relief when he realized his dad and Tyler might need a few stitches but were still very much alive and well. He also heard a yelp from Salt as someone saw to her injuries.

Over the next few minutes the room flooded with law enforcement from a variety of sources. They'd moved everyone away from the scene while barraging them with questions about various parts of the attack. It was acknowledged as a hate crime. Tyler's recount of the other two attacks cinched the idea. By the time they'd dug up all the information, it was obvious those that survived wouldn't be on the streets again anytime soon.

It was the wee hours of the morning before the investigation concluded. They put the house back into some kind of order before George and Tyler dropped into the dining room chairs while Micah gathered three beers from the fridge and joined them at the table. George looked at Micah with a twinkle in his eye.

"You'll be in trouble with Kenny for giving me alcohol."

Micah took a drink, struggling to keep himself from collapsing from the stress of the night. "What Kenny doesn't know won't hurt him."

George swirled the beer and got a sip before glancing at Micah. "And now that we're talking about not knowing, when were you going to tell me you were dating Tyler?"

Tyler choked as Micah struggled to come up with a response while George sat watching them. At first, Micah tried to find an excuse, but it only took a few seconds for him to arrive at the truth. It was time for his father to know, and this was no worse than any other.

"Yes, Tyler and I are dating. Have been for a while."

George looked perplexed. "Why didn't you tell me? I've been worrying you'd end up alone once I'm gone."

Micah stared at his dad and worked to see the missing pieces of the puzzle he'd been struggling with for a long time. His world began to tumble out of control then the words blurted from him. "I didn't think you'd approve. I wasn't sure how you'd take it, and you haven't been doing well. I didn't want to make the situation worse."

George sighed and the soft sound filled the room. "My fault, I suppose. Over the years, I've adjusted my views on a lot of topics. What it means to be gay — or have a gay son — would be high on the list of things I've changed my mind about in my lifetime." He shot Micah a satisfied expression. "This isn't a shock, son. You haven't been on a date in almost ten years, and you treat Tyler more like a boyfriend. So, I've had time to consider how I felt about having a gay child."

At that moment, Tyler yawned and his mouth was wide enough to swallow a calf. George chuckled. "I think it's late, and with all the drama, we need rest more than anything else." He focused on Tyler this time. "Don't be stupid and try to drive home. I'm sure Micah can share his bed." Micah's jaw dropped and his eyebrows shot up. But again, before he could reply, his father finished. "I'm not that old — or uptight. Just don't keep me up."

With that, George turned and headed to his bedroom, leaving Micah and Tyler gaping after his receding form.

Chapter Twelve

Tyler woke with Micah's thick arms around his chest. He enjoyed the thrill even more now that they could be open about their relationship. To drift awake each day in Micah's arms was a sensation he wanted to enjoy for years to come. The first times he'd stayed over it had been a little awkward. He kept expecting George to rethink his view and tell him to leave, but nothing of the sort had happened. Everyone's injuries from the home invasion were healing. They had buried Pepper, and Salt's wounds were improving. George had the most severe wounds and his recovery was taking longer than anyone else's.

Micah drew Tyler tight against his chest and slid his fingers over his ribs, teasing his erect nipples as he did. He nibbled a trail along the back of Tyler's neck then whispered. "Morning, handsome. How are you?"

He turned and smiled. "Pretty good. I woke up in this hot guy's arms." Micah slipped closer and kissed up the side of Tyler's throat. He relaxed as Micah's attention continued sending waves of pleasure through him.

Time slipped past as his feelings of arousal built. With another shift of their bodies, Micah was sitting on his chest, slowly grinding his bare ass against him.

He reveled in the expression of pleasure washing over Micah's face while the cowboy's rock-hard cock waved between them. Tyler reached up, wrapped his fist around it and stroked. The pre-cum leaked across his fingers, and with a broad smile, he brought them to his mouth and ran his tongue through the clear, wet trails running across his skin. Then he grabbed Micah's ass and tugged him close enough for his cock to almost touch Tyler's lips. He inhaled deeply and the musk that filled Tyler's senses lifted his arousal to new heights.

"Holy fuck, you smell good enough to eat," Tyler said.

Micah leaned forward and ran the head of his leaking cock over Tyler's lips. "Like that? You want to eat me, cowboy?"

Without a word, Tyler sucked the head of Micah's dick into his mouth and worked it like an all-day sucker. After a short time, the rancher was thrusting into Tyler's mouth. The sensations of Micah face-fucking him left Tyler even more excited. His cock was hard as granite. Tyler relished the sensations Micah created.

"Fuck, that feels amazing. I'm about to drop my load," Micah said.

Tyler refused to break the rhythm they had created as he urged Micah to the edge. Time lost all meaning as Tyler continued to pleasure Micah. But when he felt tremors wash through Micah's body, Tyler redoubled his efforts. Micah locked his muscles and let out a guttural moan.

"Damn."

Tyler's mouth flooded with cum and he swallowed quickly. The bitter-sweet substance filled his senses as Micah erupted inside his mouth again and again. But, eventually, Micah's last volley leaked from his lips.

The buildup of euphoria had driven Tyler close to climax. When Micah backed off him and down between his legs, Tyler grabbed his throbbing cock and stroked it as he worked for release. He got closer when Micah began to lick his balls. The sensation of Micah's tongue flickering over his nuts was the final push he needed, and a thick strand of white shot across his chest. Their passion had built in him until an enormous load covered him.

As the last convulsion squeezed the final drops of cum onto Tyler's stomach, Micah ran his tongue through the pools of white on his torso then proceeded to give Tyler a jizz-laced kiss that provided the perfect finale to their morning session. Micah melted against him as Tyler gasped for air. Eventually, he came down from the high and held Micah close.

"Damn. That was good," Micah said.

Tyler leaned in for another kiss. "It was amazing."

They cuddled for a minute before Micah sat up. "Crap! We're working the calves today. Dad will be pounding at the door in a few minutes to tell us he's ready. We gotta get moving."

Tyler chuckled and crawled out of the bed then he glanced at Micah. "We could shower together. It would be faster."

Micah glanced at him before cocking his head. "Okay, but we're just showering. No funny business. Promise?"

"I agree already. We better clean up or you can explain what all the cum is doing on us."

Micah rolled his eyes but crawled out of bed to head to the bathroom and a hot shower. A few seconds later, Tyler joined him in the glass stall. The steam curled around Tyler as the water pounded across his shoulders. The combination felt wonderful when he turned to wet his body. As they lathered each other, Tyler closed his eyes to enjoy the sensations. While they cleaned each other carefully, Tyler ran his hands down the crack of Micah's ass. After he located his rancher's tight opening, Tyler slipped his finger inside and stroked Micah. They continued their slow exploration for several minutes before Micah pulled away with a sigh.

Tyler ran his hands over Micah, smiling as he did. "It was just getting fun, party pooper."

Micah slapped him across the ass. "We don't have time for this kind of fun."

Tyler glanced at him then smiled. "Okay, but that's something we're definitely coming back to. I want more of that." He rinsed himself off, stepped out of the shower and dried with one of the plush towels available while Micah finished rinsing off. Soon they were both getting dressed for the work day, but even then, Tyler couldn't keep from admiring the muscular ass that Micah's jeans framed, just for Tyler to lust after. A knock at the bedroom shook him out of his daydreaming. When George's voice came through the door, he smiled. *Micah knows his dad.*

"Come on, boys. Time to get up. You can't spend the whole day sleeping."

Micah said, "We'll be out in a second, Dad. We're putting on our boots."

After a brief pause, George spoke again. "Okay, but hurry. The rest of the crew should be here soon." With that, Tyler looked toward the windows that faced the east and motioned to the dark gray of the predawn morning.

"I think we have time to eat before everyone else arrives. We'll be out in a few minutes," Micah said, then he turned to Tyler, who had been stroking his ass during the short conversation. In a low voice, Micah said, "And you're *not* helping."

Tyler planted a kiss on Micah's neck. "I thought you'd enjoy it."

"Of course, I did. That's why I needed you to knock it off and get dressed. I don't want to go to breakfast with a hard-on."

Tyler ignored Micah's grumbling as he finished dressing and left. He was adding milk to his cereal when Micah joined him in the kitchen. Tyler gave him a wink as they joined George at the table.

By the time Micah and Tyler had finished their breakfasts, George was mumbling and looked sour. In spite of the time taken for a quick meal, it wasn't long before Tyler stood at the corral gate where he'd led one of the horses the ranch used when working cattle. The little mare seemed excited to do what she had been trained for. Micah tied her to the fence and brought her saddle from the tack room. He was tightening the final strap when Lee drove into the driveway with a rig filled with saddled horses.

Tyler walked over and helped Lee lower the ramp that would make it easier to unload the horses. It didn't take long before they had the three they needed tied to the fence. In the faint light of morning, he saw they hadn't brought his mount. Before he could turn and ask, Lee spoke. "I have the three best working horses from the farm. Rusty isn't what you need today."

After an instant of consideration, he nodded in agreement then asked his other question, "Who's the third one for? George isn't able to ride at this point, and he has his own horse, anyway."

The pickup's back door opened and Kenny jumped out. Tyler turned to Lee and waited.

"George and I have been working with him to teach him how to ride. He wanted to help today, and I think he's ready."

"Mom said it was okay, so long as I wear a helmet," Kenny added.

Tyler shifted his gaze from one to another as he tried to organize his thoughts. After a few seconds, he realized this was a losing battle for him. He scowled at Kenny and Lee.

"He does what he's told and no more. No daredevil crap or you're walking back to the house. Got it?"

Kenny tensed but didn't cower. "Yes, sir. I've got it."

Still not pleased that he'd known nothing about this, Tyler took his mount from Lee, swung into the saddle and waited for Micah to ease up beside him. It made him realize how much he'd missed, being gone on the circuit so often that he hadn't been involved in the day-to-day running of the place. Once everything seemed in order, Micah led the group toward the first set of pens filled with cows and their babies. When they had it all set up, the mounted cowboys swept the pasture from the far side, drawing the animals closer. A few times, one of the cattle would try to slip past them, but the horses would sense the movement, leap toward the escaping animal and stop their attempt.

Tyler wondered what would happen when Kenny's horse was the one to react. He didn't have to wait long for his question to be answered. One of the older cows sensed Kenny's hesitancy and took off at a run with her calf at her side. His mount spun and plunged toward the racing animal with the quarter horse's legendary burst of speed. Tyler chewed on his lip as he waited for the cow to escape, for Kenny to fall from the horse or both.

The first few quick movements made by the gelding left Kenny holding on to the saddle horn as if his life depended upon it. By the time they'd reached the cow, Kenny was back in control. Tyler nodded his approval as the pair cut off the escapees and returned them to the herd. The rest of the quarter-mile long cattle drive was as uneventful, as he he'd hoped.

The sun beamed on them as they worked the first group of cattle into the corral. The air around them carried a faint haze of dust as hooves and boots ground the dirt into a footing with the consistency of powder. He appreciated Micah's skill at the sorting gate with the flood of animals pressing forward. In less time than one might think, the calves were herded in a single line down the chute connected to the working pens.

The first weanling lunged at the opening to find itself caught. The work crew moved into action with the routine care needed, then Micah grabbed one of the red-hot branding irons from the fire and pressed it against the calf's hip. With a bellow, it fought to escape and the acrid stench of burning hair filled the air. Tyler had never been a fan of branding but Micah's skill showed from the crisp, clean mark identifying the animal.

Micah put the iron back into the fire as the gate opened, releasing the calf. A few seconds later, it had rejoined its mother. The crew descended on the next calf, and they quickly finished what it needed. It was reunited with its mother as soon as it was released.

Tyler worked at a steady rhythm but knew he wasn't keeping up with Micah and Lee. He had no excuse for not shouldering his share of the work. With a glance at the others, he steeled himself and fell back into the task with renewed vigor. The sun beat down on them as it crept higher and the day heated. When the last calf rejoined its mother, they gathered in the shaded working area and everyone enjoyed cups of ice water from the cooler. As he sipped the cold water, Tyler realized he hadn't noticed George since early that morning. He turned to Micah, who was leaning against the heavy metal gate.

"I haven't seen your dad in a while."

Micah nodded and tilted his hat back. "He told me he was too tired. I suggested he could supervise and tell everyone what to do, but he said no."

Tyler considered asking more questions, but this time, it didn't seem like a good idea. He was happy with the way his relationship with Micah had been developing and he didn't want to jeopardize it by giving Micah suggestions about how to deal with George. Every once in a while he was smart enough to keep his mouth shut, and this would be one of those times. He finished his water and motioned toward the horses. "We have several more pastures to work. We'd better get moving before it gets any hotter."

A melody of soft groans came from the cowboys whose muscles had cooled down and stiffened, but everyone remounted and headed out to gather the cattle from the next quarter section. This group's enclosure had become overgrown with brush, most of which would have been waist-high to Tyler.

"The bull in here is protective of his ladies, so keep your heads up." Micah focused on Kenny. "I want you to stay on that ridge just this side of the fence line. I think everything will be fine, but if something happens, give the horse its head. He's a little more experienced with the cattle than you."

Kenny appeared to take the instructions with the weight of their importance and kept questions to himself. He tapped his heels against the horse's flanks and rode to where Micah had sent him. Once he had reached the spot, the others eased through the brush as they pushed the animals toward the working pens.

Tyler noticed a marked difference between these cattle and the previous ones. These were wary of the riders and kept them at a distance, with their ears flipping around like umbrellas in a strong wind. The animals' actions and apparent nerves had him keeping a constant watch on Kenny. If the bull was as skittish as the cows, they needed to be cautious, even on horseback.

"Heads up! There's the bull," Micah yelled.

Tyler's focus shifted to the dark bulk that had slipped through the brush without making much more than a ripple. His mount jumped, and a second later, the muscled animal was bearing down on them. But the bull couldn't track the horse as it squealed and dodged each time the bull swept his horns in attack. Micah galloped toward them, leaning over the saddle horn as he raced to help Tyler.

The bull disappeared into a thicket of scrub oak while the cowboys shouted suggestions. Then the animal burst from the cover — tracking Kenny at a dead run, who froze with his mouth dropped open, clenching onto the reins as if the thin strips of leather would somehow save him.

Tyler was the first to realize what was happening. "Kenny! Drop the reins. Drop the reins!"

The kid's attention snapped to Tyler, but the order didn't break him from his stupor. The gelding Kenny rode bolted for the pens several hundred yards across the broken and hazard-covered area. The bull's bellow sent chills through Tyler's spine. All three of them spun, racing in pursuit of the youngster who clung for his life to the mane of his rangy, quick-footed gelding. Then Micah yelled instructions.

"It's a trap pen we put in a few years ago. Turn the bull to the right and we can catch him while Kenny escapes out the other side. But we have to close the gap between us."

Tyler leaned forward, his face almost buried in his horse's mane. He sensed Lee and Micah right behind him. They shortened the distance and shifted through the open gate. Tyler breathed a quick sigh of relief when Kenny turned to the right and plunged into the catch pen.

Whether Kenny had heard him or it was dumb luck, the results were a break for Tyler.

Kenny found the exit and ducked through it as the bull barreled into the pen and roared his frustration at his victim eluding him. Lee shoved the gate closed behind the heels of Tyler and Micah's mounts. The experienced riders with their well-trained horses soon had the bull worked into a small side enclosure.

Once he was certain the herd's sire was secure, Tyler turned to check on Kenny. It took a few seconds to find the youngster, but once he did, he couldn't keep from being sympathetic. Kenny stood, hands on his knees, emptying his stomach into the tall grass.

Today was sure a learning experience for him and he did good. Now we'll see if he really wants to be here.

Chapter Thirteen

A late fall heat wave drove Tyler to the dim cool of the tack building. The thick concrete blocks used in its construction kept the interior several degrees cooler, and with both doors open, it was almost as comfortable as the air-conditioned house. If the temperature climbed, even this haven would be hot by mid-afternoon. But, at this point, it was a comfortable place to give him time to reflect.

To keep his hands busy, he decided to clean a working saddle from their assortment. He gathered the saddle soap, along with a bucket of warm water and a few cloths he kept for this purpose. He dampened one of the rags and carefully cleaned the leather. Once that was accomplished, he loaded the saddle soap onto a clean, damp cloth then worked it into the tanned hide. The smells of saddle soap and leather filled the room as he buffed each area to a low shine before moving to the next section. The scents merged in ways that brought back the comforting feeling of his childhood memories.

All those factors combined for Tyler to make this his favorite escape from the rest of the ranch.

"Tyler! Tyler, you in here?"

But so much for my quiet spot.

He sighed. "I'm cleaning a saddle, Mom. Come in."

Tyler made a final swipe before laying down his cloth and turning to his mother. He hid his expression as she squinted into the room, getting used to the dimness. Once she was adjusted, she swung toward Tyler.

"I figured I'd find you in the pouting shed."

Tyler rolled his eyes, cringing at his mother's term for his retreat. "I'm not moping, Mother, just getting some quiet time."

She studied him then held out her hand. "Give me a rag and I'll help."

Without questioning, Tyler handed her one of the cloths and they worked on the saddle together. Several minutes passed in a silence, which he found calmed him almost as much as the room itself. Another gust of wind hit the door and tossed a thin coating of dust across the floor.

"How's Kenny after the bull drama?" Mary Lou asked in a conversational tone.

As he recalled the youngster, Tyler couldn't help but chuckle. "He came back, so that's good. But he's been careful around the cattle. He'll be fine after a little more time. Lee told him he could ride a horse once he's comfortable with them again."

"Good. Glad he's working out his issues."

The quiet captured the room once more as they lifted out another saddle and set to work on it. He pulled out a cinch strap and found it whole and blemish-free. He let it slide between his fingers, checking every inch, verifying that it was as sound as when it had been new.

"It's exhausting to question everything. How often do you check it?" Mary Lou asked.

Tyler peered at his mother but couldn't stop himself from snorting. *She knows me too well.* "I check it all the time. Sometimes I feel like stopping halfway through a run to check it again."

"Have you found any more times someone tampered with it?"

Tyler shook his head. "Not really..."

Mary Lou's sculpted brow lifted. "Nothing?"

Tyler paused, his lips twisting back and forth a few times before answering, "A time or two there might have been a little damage, but it could have been wear."

"Keep an eye on it. Better safe than sorry."

Tyler nodded in agreement but kept his peace otherwise as they checked the saddle. The comfortable silence had settled around them when the actual purpose of her search to find him finally became clear—although it wasn't terribly surprising.

"How are things between you and Micah? He told George that he was gay."

Tyler eased to a stop then studied his mother. "I didn't pressure him into doing anything. George figured it out when those people broke into their house."

She chuckled. "Oh, sweetie. George has known for years but he wanted Micah to come to him. He wasn't any happier about Micah being forcibly outed. But you didn't answer my question."

Tyler made another attempt at diversion. "What's that?"

"Oh, don't try the clueless routine with me. You aren't good at it."

"Fine. Things are going all right. We're both busy, and that means we don't get to be together as much as we'd like."

She patted Tyler's shoulder. "Both of you have a lot on your plate. Between your rodeo circuit and the care that George needs, I can see how your schedule is crazy." Mary Lou paused and considered her son. "You also need to realize that the time may come when you're forced to choose between your two loves."

Tyler chuckled a little at his drama-filled mother. "As melodramatic as that sounds, it won't be an issue. We may be busy but we're managing. We work with each other and know the other person has a ton of things going on, too."

Mary Lou pursed her lips. "Not everyone is as blunt as you are. It'd be good to remember that."

Tyler bristled, but tried to keep his response civil. "Tell me one time I did that."

"Okay, how about when you came out?"

"Well, I *was* thirteen when that happened, which should buy me a little latitude, but I thought I handled it with a great deal of subtlety."

Mary Lou's laughter verged on hysterical and it took time before she reached the point where speaking was a possibility again.

"Your recollection of that event is not even close to what I remember."

"And what is your memory?" Tyler asked.

"I recall a young man who had worked himself up to tell me. You had your arms folded across your chest as you stood in my bedroom. You took a couple of deep breaths and belted out. 'I'm gay. I like dudes. If you can't deal with that then you need to change your mind.' That's the bluntness I'm talking about."

Tyler frowned, but inside he relived the moment from his past and found his mother's recall of the event was accurate. He still refused to acknowledge that his mother was right.

"It was one of the major events in my life. I think I handled it well."

This time when Tyler met his mother's gaze, what he saw softened his heart. She'd been his champion for as long as he could remember. In spite of the teasing, she would always be at his side.

She popped the white cloth across the saddle and motioned toward Tyler. "Grab another one and I'll show you how to do it right. You've got to take care of your equipment, keep it spotless and working at top efficiency." She paused for a second and winked at him. "You've heard me so many times it's embedded in you. I'm sure your trailer is immaculate and ready to head out to your next rodeo. A man of your position has to be ready to leave at a moment's notice. Where is your next competition?"

Tyler felt like a kid who hadn't done his chores before his after-school snack and cartoons. The last place he wanted his mother was in his trailer—which hadn't had a thorough cleaning recently. If she saw the current state of his living quarters, he'd never hear the end of it. He decided to try to answer the part of her question about his next rodeo and avoid the rest of the topic.

"The next one's in Kansas City this weekend. We're hoping Micah will come with me. It'll depend on how George is doing but Kenny already has a *Harry Potter* and *X-Men* marathon planned."

"George likes those movies?"

"I don't know but he agreed."

Mary Lou nodded and said. "That young man is there more than at his own home."

Tyler considered his interaction with Kenny over the past few months. "He's settled in. He's a different kid from the one who threw firecrackers at the horses in the Independence Day parade. And the level he and George have bonded is crazy. He treats Kenny like another son."

She set the cleaning tools aside. "That's enough buffing the tack. I have several things on my to-do list for today and I don't want to be late for dinner at your RV tonight. I can't wait to see the touches you've added that made the place yours."

Tyler swallowed hard, trying to find an escape hatch. "What? Dinner?"

"The dinner to show off your beautiful home to your mother. Raid the pantry and freezer at the lodge. There should be some nice steaks." She shot him a glowing smile and headed for the exit. With a pause at the doorway, she nodded at Tyler. "I can't wait. Don't worry about the wine, either. I'll pick out something that will go with the meal."

Well, that strategy didn't work. Now I've got a different kind of cleaning to do — and fast.

* * * *

The evening air had the nip of early winter as Micah helped Tyler get ready for his first run at his most recent event. He'd had reservations about taking the trip but his dad had insisted he go. *Might be your last chance to get away, he told me.* It wasn't as if Micah didn't want to go, but he couldn't keep depending on other people to keep the farm going while he was off tagging after Tyler.

But he'd enjoyed their trip and needed a break from the pressures of the ranch and George's illness. His dad was finishing the last rounds of chemo and radiation. The wait to hear the latest test results was something none of them enjoyed with. So, Micah had every reason to take advantage of a final trip.

"Hey, hand me that."

Micah glanced up at Tyler's vague instructions. "The blanket?"

Tyler gave him a blank expression before obviously realizing what he had said—or how unclear he'd been. "Yeah, sorry. Kind of distracted, I guess."

"Don't worry," Micah said. "You should be focused on your next run."

Tyler shook his head as he tossed the saddle pad in place. "I'm having trouble getting my thoughts together. I can't get myself in order today."

"Do what Carl told you. Focus on the arrow."

Tyler chuckled. "You're sounding like Carl. I must have talked about him a lot."

"It was an important week. You should think about what he told you, decide where everything fits."

Micah chuckled when Tyler rolled his eyes.

Then Tyler grinned and stuck out his tongue at him. "You don't have to always be the adult."

Micah considered a response when he sensed someone join them. He glanced over to find Everett. *Why does he have both horses? He has to know Tyler doesn't like for anyone else to touch Rusty these days. Even I leave prepping Rusty to Tyler, unless he tells me otherwise.* But Everett *had* brought in both animals. Micah expected Tyler to explode, but to his surprise, he didn't react.

Tyler took the reins. "Thanks, Everett. I'll take care of him."

Micah questioned how well he knew Tyler, but then noticed Tyler was gripping the leather leads hard enough to make his knuckles pale. Without a word, Micah moved to the trailer and carried Tyler's saddle to where he stood. A few feet away he stopped and tilted it toward Tyler to give him a good chance to inspect the underside. Micah's reward was the smile Tyler gave him, but he still double-checked everything before taking the gear from Micah and throwing it over Rusty's back.

Tyler moved with practiced ease to adjust the tack. Once he'd secured everything, Tyler relocated Rusty to a tie-out. He gave Everett room beside Rusty to secure his mount as he came to have a final quiet moment with Micah.

He leaned in and gave Tyler a quick peck. "Good luck, but you're so talented that there's no luck involved."

Tyler returned the gentle kiss and patted Micah's cheek. The touch wound its way through Micah and set his body tingling. Then he realized Tyler hadn't stopped talking. "Thanks for the vote of confidence. It's just that the issue with the straps has me keyed up."

Micah stepped to Rusty and ran his hands over every piece of gear on Tyler's horse. Other than an odd wet spot, the tack was sound and whole. He turned to Tyler and winked. "Not a cut in the entire setup. You should be good."

The announcer began listing the steer wrestling pairs for round one and Tyler's was an early run. Their gazes met, but this time, there was only silence as Tyler and Everett mounted and eased their way to the gates. They walked their horses until they disappeared into the dim recesses of the stadium. Once Micah knew for certain that neither of them would race back for something he could help with, Micah made his way to the grandstands and found an excellent seat close to the action.

Micah sat taking in the sights of the largest arena he'd ever been inside. There were multiple levels and a maze of concrete behind the seating. It probably wasn't as impressive as he imagined but was simply outside his experience. As he continued to study the enormous venue, he realized a couple of his fingers were burning. He lifted his hand and the tips of two fingers were the color of a ripe tomato. And to add to his panic, in a spot where the burn was intense, a small blister had appeared. When the pain ratcheted up several degrees, Micah decided that getting whatever was on him off was more important than a primo seat.

He scrambled down the row, shot out into one of the main tunnels and spotted what he had been searching for — a bathroom. Micah ran to the sink and opened the water until a torrent washed over his hands. He rinsed off his fingers then soaped them in quick succession. He breathed a sigh of relief when the pain lessened then stopped. But he continued washing until his fingers were back to their normal color.

After doing a few more rinses, Micah raced out of the bathroom, hoping he hadn't missed Tyler's first round. His heart sank when he rounded a corner as the crowd exploded with thunderous applause. But then he realized the pair in the arena wasn't Tyler and Everett.

He glanced around and found he'd lost his original seat, but he spotted a vacancy a few rows farther up. After some maneuvering, he had a seat where he could again watch everything. Micah made himself comfortable as a steer released. He held his focus only long enough to note the next bulldogger rode a Paint, not Rusty's familiar solid chestnut. He leaned back and enjoyed watching without the personal investment he would have had if it were Tyler. By the time the cowboy was dusting his jeans off, he had turned in a strong ride, but Micah thought Tyler could do better.

As the arena was being set up for the next contestant, Micah saw who he was waiting for—Tyler. But then he noticed Rusty twist and turn as Tyler rode toward the starting box. He shouldn't have as many difficulties accomplishing the same maneuver he'd done hundreds of times before. Micah tried to figure out the reason for Rusty's difficult attitude but couldn't find a cause.

After Tyler seemed to ignore the horse's conduct, both riders positioned themselves and the tension soaked into Micah as they waited. Then the round burst into action.

The steer leaped from the chute and raced for the opposite end of the arena and escape. The horses galloped into pursuit, each hoof-fall leaving a whirl of powder in its wake. Tyler shift his body in a way Micah had never seen before. Something was wrong, but Micah didn't know what. Tyler leaned forward, and this time, there was a collective gasp from the crowd as the saddle twisted sideways and everyone knew Tyler was in trouble. Micah held his breath as Tyler launched himself at the running steer. As soon as Tyler left his back, Rusty slid to a stop with the saddle dangling in the dust.

With his timing wrecked, Tyler struggled to hold the animal, much less throw him. He skidded a few yards before he could regain his footing. The powdered earth boiled up on either side as Tyler tried to power his way into throwing the steer with no level of finesse. It took longer, but with a straining of every muscle in Tyler's body, the calf rolled and landed on his back.

An instant after the round ended, Tyler sprinted to Rusty, who stood with his head drooping and the gear hanging under his belly. He grabbed the reins, pulled off the saddle and tossed it over one shoulder before leading his mount to the exit. Micah flew down the stairs, trying to intercept Tyler and find a way to help. It took a few seconds of searching, but he found Tyler checking the cinch with Rusty tied beside him. His expression was one of anger and confusion as he glanced at Micah.

"It broke! It was fine two minutes before I started and now..." He thrust the torn part of the strap toward Micah, his eyes begging for confirmation. Micah studied it carefully and agreed. The new leather strap had torn like the material had dry-rotted. Then Micah noticed the dampness on the leather. He touched the tips of his fingers against the material then rubbed them against each other. A few seconds later a faint stinging started, and the clues came together.

"Tyler. Check Rusty where this break was and see if there's a sore."

Tyler shot him a quizzical expression but moved the horse to search for a wound. As Rusty was being evaluated, Micah caught movement from the corner of his eye — Everett leaving the pen. Micah shot his hand out and grabbed the reins of Everett's horse. "I think you'll want to stick around for this bit of drama. Tyler's going to want to chat with you in a minute."

"What the hell?" Tyler said.

"Big blister, right?"

"Yeah, the size of my thumb. How'd you know?"

Micah held out his hand. "I have my version of it from touching the strap before you got on Rusty."

"What is it?"

"Some kind of acid is my guess. But I think our friend Everett could tell us more about it." He looked toward the hazer.

"I don't know what you're talking about. You have no evidence I'm responsible for any of this," Everett said.

"I may not have proof, but I'd bet the police will be very interested," Tyler said as he dialed nine-one-one. Before he finished giving the operator the information, two uniformed police arrived and pulled Everett to the side to question him. Micah ran through the sequence of happenings with the cops. When the officers reviewed the events, they searched the area and found a plastic syringe in the trash, still holding a few drops of a fluid. They put it in an evidence packet. It didn't take long to write the statements and Everett was being stuffed into the back of a police car.

One of the officers who'd arrived first came back to them. "We located a bigger bottle in his pickup, but he's not talking. The only thing he said to us was that he wants an attorney present for any interrogation. If we have questions relevant to the investigation, we will be back in contact with you. We have your information."

Tyler nodded but added nothing else. To Micah, he seemed defeated. There was a little more conversation exchanged before the police returned to their routes on the fairgrounds. Tyler sat on an upturned bucket as if the world was close to ending.

"I'm finished. It will be a long time before Rusty can tolerate a saddle again. If Everett's goal was to ruin me, he succeeded. I guess he used a stronger version of the acid this time. It's never caused anything like blisters before. But regardless, I'm screwed."

"Could you find a replacement horse?" Micah asked.

"Maybe, but a good bulldogging pony's tough to find."

A young woman riding to them leading another horse broke Micah's train of thought. He started to direct her away when Tyler's face lit up and he burst out. "Gracie?"

"*Kaheé*. Good to see you again."

"What are you doing so far from Montana?"

She shrugged. "Uncle said he felt it was the right time to take a trip south and check on you."

Tyler opened and closed his mouth a few times before pressing his lips tight together. Micah decided he could step in and rescue Tyler. He held out his hand at the striking woman. "Hi, my name's Micah. I'm guessing you are the Gracie that Tyler talks about all the time."

She shot Micah a dazzling smile and returned his grip. "And you must be the boyfriend. Tyler's right. You *are* hot."

Micah's face flashed red, and when he glanced toward Tyler, he'd turned a color mimicking a cardinal in winter. But through the whole encounter, she was laughing at their discomfort. Neither of them knew what to say for a few seconds then Gracie said, "He also thought you might want someone you're comfortable with riding hazer for you. I brought the horse you'd been using, too. It seemed kind of dumb to drive across the country only to find out something had happened to your ride."

This time when she finished, Tyler had a reply ready. "I'm thrilled you're here, and as usual, Carl knew the help I needed." He gave her a quick summary of what had just happened with Everett. "But it won't be long before it's my go again. You braced for some action?"

Her satisfaction seemed to grow and it washed over both of them. "We've been in the trailer for days. All three of us are ready for a little sprint to work out the stiffness." Gracie turned to Micah as she handed the reins for the big piebald she led to Tyler. "You'll want your seat in the stands. It shouldn't take more than a few minutes to wrap up this rodeo and have some jingle in our pockets."

"You might be a little optimistic. My first round ended with my saddle dragging under my horse."

She chuckled. "You had your hazer working against you, and now Rocky and I are here to make sure everything is perfect for you to win."

Micah couldn't help but laugh at Gracie's enthusiasm. Winning appeared to be an expectation, not a wish, and her certainty became contagious. Tyler swung onto the horse Gracie had brought him. The two of them trotted for the pens and the beginning of the second round. After they disappeared from sight, Micah sped back to the bleachers and found an empty seat not far from his earlier one. With the near disaster having just passed, he'd take anything that felt like a change in Tyler's luck. There had been Gracie's miraculous arrival. That was a mystery he had no idea how to begin unraveling. *Carl must have some pretty impressive powers of intuition.*

The steer wrestlers worked their way through until Tyler and Gracie were readying themselves. Tyler's mount had more fire to his disposition than anything Micah had seen with Rusty. It reared a few times and squealed with Tyler clinging to him like a tick on a bloodhound.

That horse isn't poorly trained. It's excited.

Both riders moved into place and Micah clenched his fingers around the metal bench in a death grip. A heartbeat later, Tyler bobbed his head and the tableaux burst into action. Gracie rode like someone born on horseback. She was an extension of the animal and only a fraction of a second passed before the steer was positioned in just the right spot. Tyler's approach was more of a pounding attack but his position was perfect and his lunge reminded Micah of a mountain lion dropping on its prey from above. In the blink of an eye, Tyler wrapped his arms through the steer's horns. With a few well-paced maneuvers done in the blink of an eye, the animal had four legs in the air. At that point, Micah pumped his fist and cheered. A second later the bleachers exploded with a standing ovation.

Things were improving.

Finally.

Chapter Fourteen

Tyler rocked in the saddle as the weakening rays of sun painted his back with its slight warmth. Bullwinkle still had the habit of lunging in the box but now he knew why the horse behaved as it did during the competition. Tyler maintained it was the animal's new name, but it was the classic pairing with Gracie's Rocky. In the time since the altercation with Everett, a lot had changed. His former hazer's current living quarters were in the county jail, awaiting trial. He continued to refuse to confess to any crime surrounding the sabotage of Tyler's gear, but in hearing some of the stories coming out, it seemed pretty obvious that his professed indifference to Tyler being gay had been a complete sham. That, coupled with the fact that his position on the team was secondary in importance, seemed to give Everett all the reason he needed to try to hurt Tyler. But even though he had refused to confess, tests confirmed the liquid was an acid that targeted leather. The combination made for a slam dunk case against him.

The changes were for the best. At the competitions following Everett's arrest, Gracie had proven to be an amazing hazer. His scores had improved from their first event together. *Now? Well, I'm riding better than I have in a long time. I'm not sure how much of it is me improving and what part is having a partner who isn't trying to ruin my career. I hope someday to really understand why Everett hates me the way he does, just because I'm living as who I really am.*

Tyler soon stopped dissecting the issues with Everett. Gracie had to be one of the best horsemen Tyler had worked with, including Carl. He'd offered to share his living space with her, but she had turned him down with a smile. She told him she preferred the tent and bedroll she'd brought with her. Her next words shook him out of his introspection.

"We're up next."

He grinned at Gracie. "You enjoy outdoing the boys."

She returned his smile. "I don't mind whipping them. It's a nice side effect."

This time Tyler grew serious. "Why are you here? I'd think you'd have other things to do than rescue me."

She shrugged as they walked the horse's closer. But to his surprise, she gave him an answer. "Uncle asked me to check on you. It's a good idea to keep Uncle happy."

Tyler nodded as the animals picked up their speed toward the opening gate and their last run. While they could still hear each other, she twisted in the saddle and said, "This is the make it or break it round. Be sure about your focus. Remember the buffalo hunt."

I remember how Carl used the Crow tradition of hunting buffalo from horseback to teach me the finer points of steer wrestling. He flashed her a nod of understanding and backed his mount into the box. A few seconds later, the steer shot forward and Tyler fell into his routine. Their timing as a team was perfection and the results seemed foretold. Afterward, they trotted the horses through the pens and to the trailer. They dismounted and tethered their mounts before Tyler grabbed Gracie and spun her in a circle.

"That was it! We were faster than the next team by at least a full second. That must have qualified us for National Finals."

Gracie nodded in agreement as he set her back on the ground. "It was a good run, one of best this season." She paused for a moment and winked at Tyler. "Uncle has been keeping track of your scores."

"Not me alone. It took both of us — and I'm grateful," Tyler said.

She smiled but unsaddled her horse and stored its tack in the trailer. Tyler focused on duplicating Gracie's effort when he heard his name called. He turned and spotted the bull rider and his husband — Dustin and Shane. After saving him from the attack earlier in the summer, these two had a special place in Tyler's heart. He stepped up to each of them and shook their hands. Tyler paused a second to give Gracie an opportunity to introduce herself, but when she chose otherwise, he respected her wishes. He glanced back to the men. "What's up? I thought Laramie was your next stop?"

"We still are..." Dustin started but then he glanced at Shane before trying to explain again. "We were at Micah's ranch this morning. He had some bull calves he hoped we might be interested in buying." Dustin dwindled off and Shane took up the conversation thread.

"We got there and Micah acted distracted. After a while, we asked if we should come back another day. He seemed to be barely hanging on to keep from having a breakdown."

Dustin continued, "After a minute or two, he tried to explain what was happening and we agreed that his stuff was a lot more important to deal with."

"He didn't want to tell you because he was afraid the news would screw up the winning streak you're having. He doesn't want to cause you problems," Shane said.

By now, Tyler had become frustrated at the confusing information from Dustin and Shane. "What? What's the big crisis?"

They fell silent for a minute then Shane said, "Micah's dad is in bad shape. The doctor gives him a day or two. We thought you should know, and this didn't seem like phone call kind of information."

Tyler stood in shock, trying to bring his thoughts together. *Why didn't he tell me? I would have been there for them.* But he came to himself and realized they were waiting for his reaction. Even Gracie seemed to be listening for his response. After a few deep breaths, he turned to Dustin. "How bad is it? Do I have time to get home?"

He shrugged. "It isn't like anyone can tell you an exact second. But from our conversation, Micah's dad won't be around for much longer."

Tyler surveyed his surroundings, gathering his thoughts as he tried to decide what would be the best thing he could do. Then Gracie said, "The next rodeo is a few weeks off and I'm close enough to visit the family. I'll take care of the horses so you don't have to worry about them."

Tyler acknowledged Gracie's gift with a nod then turned back to the others. "Thanks for letting me know. I've got to go home and see if I can help Micah. I gotta…"

Shane nodded and picked up the conversation. "You can fill us in later. Go do what you need to do."

Tyler set his jaw in resolve, and with everyone's help, he was soon cutting down the miles between him and his goal. He knew it would be a long drive and hoped it wouldn't be too late. Hours into the trip, the dark loneliness had him questioning so many choices he'd made over the past months while he and Micah had begun their relationship—or at least *he* had fallen in love with the hot rancher. That was his greatest revelation as he pressed through the night and toward his goal. *I love Micah.* He also understood that the days of seeing each other when they could work it in had to come to an end.

Hours later, Tyler sighed in relief when he passed the marker for the Oklahoma state line. With every window down so the cool night air would help keep him awake, he focused on reaching Micah. As the mile markers rolled past, dawn fought its way back from the black coils of darkness. The stark, rolling hills melded their way to the growing urban sprawl surrounding the state's center. By the time Tyler reached his goal, the first kiss of color showed on the objects around him as he came to a stop in front of Micah's home.

The house loomed silent and dark, which wasn't normal. Micah always rose before the sun, and by now, George would be making breakfast. None of that was happening this morning. Tyler steeled himself to what he would discover. As he pulled in, he noticed his mother's pickup parked to one side. He made his way to the entrance, surprised to find it unlocked, given the recent, almost fatal, break-in.

Tyler moved through the door, careful not to disturb anyone. As he slipped into the living room, he heard someone coming down the hall. A second or two later Micah came stumbling into the dim space. He stopped in the middle of the room in his briefs, scrubbed his eyes then stared at him. "Tyler?"

"Yeah. I got here as soon as I could. Am I too late?"

Micah rubbed his eyes again and yawned. "Too late for what? Sorry, but I haven't gotten much sleep and I'm having trouble following you."

Tyler nodded and gathered his thoughts before beginning again. "I ran into Dustin and Shane last night. They said they were here and that George had taken a turn for the worse." His voice dropped and tears formed in the corner of his eyes. "They said he wasn't expected to live long. I wanted to be here for you."

Tyler stepped forward and took Micah into his arms. Micah stiffened but then leaned into him. They embraced until he felt Micah relax and pull away. But Micah kept his hand on his arm as their eyes met then Micah began to explain.

"The guys must have gotten confused about who was getting worse. One of our best bulls was fading and we had to put him down late yesterday. It isn't the same prognosis for Dad. He isn't out of the woods, but the doctor tells us he has stabilized. But with all the emotional upheaval, I can see how they might have gotten confused. I'm sure I was a wreck. Dad's had about as much support as anyone could wish for between your mom, Kenny and everyone else who's been coming by to help, but to paraphrase Mark Twain, news of his death is greatly exaggerated."

The fear and tension drained from Tyler's system. His emotions swung from elation to anger but the cold tinge of what could have been was the most dominant. "I can't do this anymore. I just can't. I thought George was dying and I wasn't there to support you."

"Oh, Tyler, I'd love for us to be together, but I have to be here for Dad."

Tyler shook his head and struggled to explain what he was proposing. "No. I'm not asking you to travel with me. I want to stay here with you. I love you, Micah. I can't let this happen again. I have to be with you." He drew Micah close, touched their lips together and delicious electricity washed across Tyler.

Micah tightened his grip as they gazed at one another. Tyler felt him tremble and Micah crushed their lips back together. The heat of the moment left its effect on Tyler. Their kiss stretched out as the passion built with each passing heartbeat. Each place Micah touched left a spot of pleasurable fire.

Micah traced the tip of his finger over Tyler's lips then slipped away. "We keep this up and we won't get much else done. I wanted to stop long enough to tell you that I love you, too, but I'm not asking you to give up your first love to be with me."

Tyler considered Micah's statement then replied. "Last spring, I might have thought I loved bulldogging more than anything else. I had a passion for the sport and an aptitude that made it potentially something I could make a living doing. But when you came along, I found out what it means to love someone. Last night as I drove through the pitch darkness like a mad man to be here when you needed me, I knew who I loved and where I had to be."

"Oh. I don't know what to say. I thought the most we could hope for from a relationship—"

Tyler stopped Micah's rambling with another kiss. Once they locked eyes again, he smiled. "I've been driving way too long and there is no way I could have a talk that makes any sense. Let's rest, and over the next few days, we can figure out how we want our lives to go." Micah started to argue but Tyler waved him into silence. "Even if I were to change my mind, there's no other competition for two weeks and Gracie went back to Montana to visit her family and took the horses with her. So, I've got no hazer and no horse. That gives us a perfect time to decide which house we'll live in until we can get our own place built."

"Or you could let me help you find a house close to here."

Tyler spun to see his mother standing at the hallway wrapped in a thick sleeping robe.

"Since I'm the only Realtor in this crew," she went on.

"Or they could take over this ranch. It'll all go to Micah at some point, anyway." George emerged from his room as he continued. "And I have no intentions of cashing in my ticket soon, in spite of what your friends told you."

Tyler and Micah glanced from one parent to the other, overwhelmed. Micah rolled his eyes and said, "Well, shit."

* * * *

Years later

A breath of early spring morning chilled air curled through the cabin and unfurled across Tyler's exposed butt. He cuddled closer to Micah and tucked the bedding around them to prevent any more wisps of cold from robbing him of the heat that he and Micah generated. At first, Micah grumbled at being disturbed from his warm spot, but soon they were again tight against each other, and Tyler spent the quiet minutes reliving the highlights of their wedding the previous day. The small ceremony had been perfect for the two of them. To top off the celebration, the weather had been perfect, with a glorious blue sky and enough nip to the air to remind everyone that it was spring in Montana.

Today's weather already had all the signs of being equally beautiful. But more important than the outstanding weather was the sexy man whose arms had been wrapped around him when he'd awakened. He and Micah had been living together for several years now. They'd been talking about a wedding for months and had come to the same conclusion – 'What the heck. Let's make this thing official.'

Everything had been progressing well until Tyler had told his mother about their plan to wed. Once Mary Lou had found out her baby was getting married, the world had shifted on its axis. As George had explained it, she'd become more than a little unhinged. On the upside, none of her special touches would have cost Tyler and Micah anything beyond a few items they had insisted they would choose and pay for themselves. As co-owner of their combined ranches, Tyler didn't make as much as he had when he'd been bulldogging. But now he woke up every morning with the love of his life. The tradeoff had been a no-brainer. But his mother had gone far beyond any reasonable limits, and by the time she'd planned white peacocks to wander around during the ceremony, they'd known they'd lost all control of their own wedding. Even George had become a little nuts and had joined Mary Lou's horde.

The saving stroke of luck had come when Tyler had made the call to invite Carl to the ceremony. Good fortune graced Tyler. He'd caught Carl at home and in a chatty mood. As Tyler recounted the insane direction the wedding had taken, Carl had laughed more often than anything else. His mirthful response hadn't been a surprise to Tyler, but what he hadn't been expecting was a solution. Carl had suggested a way to save the situation—have the wedding in Montana. As Carl had pointed out, only the most determined of the attendees would weather the trip to his home. *'We might even make some of the directional landmarks disappear for anyone you want to be certain doesn't make it to the festivities.'*

Micah had been easy to convince, but when Carl had added the possibility of a vacation cabin, it had become too good to be true. The honeymoon cottage made the plans perfect. His mother still had some of her special touches but the ceremony had become very much what he and Micah had envisioned. And just to make it even more perfect, both really and spiritually, Carl had offered to officiate. When Gracie and Kenny had agreed to stand up for Tyler and Micah had asked Lee to be his best man, the last of the details had fallen into place.

From the wedding to the intimate reception afterward, it had been perfection. Gracie had talked a drum circle into performing and Tyler had found them an amazing addition. While it hadn't been an enormous wedding, it had been a celebration to satisfy everyone involved.

After partying until late into the night, they'd arrived at the cabin and had found it more amazing than they'd imagined. The rustic decor helped create the perfect setting. But as tired as they had been, all they'd managed was to light the wood-burning stove, strip and fall asleep in each other's arms.

"What're you doing?"

Tyler turned to his newly minted husband and drew him in for a lingering kiss. He slid the tips of his fingers over Micah's short beard before answering, "Damn, you are *so* sexy."

Micah nibbled on Tyler's earlobe before placing a strip of kisses down his neck. It didn't take long before they became more urgent and Tyler slid his hands over Micah's bare chest. They continued until Micah sank into the bedding with a long sigh.

"If we're going any further, someone will need to stoke the stove and warm up this place," Micah said.

"You saying you want my good bits out in this freezing room?"

Micah winked at him. "I promise to make it worth the effort."

His husband yelped when Tyler kicked the blankets off both of them and scooted to the edge of the bed while Micah tugged the covers back into place. The nip in the cabin encouraged Tyler to move fast and spread a handful of kindling across the exposed coals they'd banked last night before crawling under the thick layer of blankets. In a few minutes, he had a fire crackling then raced back to bed. Micah welcomed him with a flick of the covers and a twinkle in his eyes – until Tyler slid into the bed and stuck his frigid feet against Micah.

"Damn!" Micah yelled. "You're freezing-ass cold. Oh my God!"

Tyler chuckled and held Micah against him. A few seconds later, he stopped trying to escape as Tyler warmed. A little longer and Micah snuggled back tight and sighed. "Okay, you get to keep living with me but you better *never* do that to me again."

Tyler made his eyes wide and innocent. "Oh, no, I'd *never* do that again. It would just be *too* mean."

Micah chuckled before leaning down and running his tongue over Tyler's hard nipple. When he yelped and grabbed Micah, he laughed. "Don't mess with me, big boy."

"Oh? And should I be worried?"

Tyler curved around the hot rancher and slowly ran his hands over Micah, losing himself in the delicious texture. As they relaxed in gentle exploration, Tyler piled pillows behind him and pulled Micah so he sat between Tyler's legs. With the room reaching a balmy temperature, Tyler flipped the comforter off them then drank in the handsome man laid out before him.

"Damn, you're so fucking hot," Tyler said.

Micah twisted toward Tyler until their lips touched. The caress spread heat over Tyler like a scorching summer day. He returned the kiss, each point of contact bringing Tyler to increasing heights of arousal. After they explored each other for several minutes, Micah pulled away and ran his hand over Tyler's face. The gentle caress left Tyler swimming in contentment. Tyler returned the gesture with a touch on Micah's jaw that let him enjoy the texture of Micah's immaculately groomed beard, which had always been an attraction for him. A few seconds later he realized Micah waited in silence.

Tyler brushed his thumb over Micah's lips then studied his husband. "What? I know you're up to something."

Micah lunged in and planted a quick kiss on the tip of Tyler's nose before speaking. "Well…as much as I love enjoying my beefy man, I'm in the mood to give him something more like sausage."

It took Tyler a second to translate Micah's weird declaration, then his face broke into an all-encompassing chuckle. "A little wiener-sharing sounds amazing." They moved slowly, touching and tasting each other until they had positioned themselves where they wanted. Micah's hard cock was inches from Tyler's mouth. As he flicked his tongue over Micah's leaking member, Micah swallowed Tyler's hard length until it was buried and his lips were rubbing against his bush. He savored the waves of pleasure until all he thought of was the euphoria coursing through his body.

Tyler was shaken from his stupor when Micah wiggled beside him, reminding Tyler that Micah wanted to share the pleasure of their lovemaking. Tyler gave a nod then refocused on giving Micah enough pleasure to send him into a climax that would forever be part of his memories of their wedding. He wrapped his fist around Micah's dick and used his tongue to lick it like a snow cone in the middle of an Oklahoma summer. As Tyler flickered his tongue over Micah's steel-hard shaft, the taste of pre-cum and musk filled his senses. The combination had Tyler filled with the layers of bliss he experienced each time he made love with Micah.

An instant later, Micah fingered his hole. Tyler's body trembled as Micah worked the first joint of his finger inside him and began sliding it in and out as he continued sucking Tyler's cock. The combination of delightful sensations left him quivering with pleasure as he lost himself in the sensation. Several minutes later he was yanked from his lust-fueled trance by a stinging slap on his ass.

Tyler yelped and turned to Micah, but before he could ask, Micah said, "I plan to fuck that tight-muscled ass until you remember what I did every time you sit down for the next week."

Tyler rolled to his stomach and wiggled his butt in the air. "Come on, stud. Let's see what you got."

Micah jumped behind Tyler and pulled his cheeks apart. Tyler moved to his knees with his chest against the bed to open himself for what Micah proposed. Micah leaned down, planting a kiss on each of Tyler's ass cheeks. As he moved lower, Micah pried his butt open then pressed his face into Tyler's crack and ran his tongue over Tyler's puckered butthole. By the time he'd repeated the action several times, Tyler had buried his face into the pillow and his moans filled the cabin with the sounds of his pleasure. Micah worked his tongue into Tyler's hole, tongue-fucking him until Tyler couldn't contain himself.

"Shit, you have me ready. I need dick and I need it *now*," Tyler said.

He heard the lube snap open and Micah began coating his asshole. Before long, the finger-fucking Micah was giving him had him way past ready for his thick cock. "Come on. Stop teasing. Put it in."

Seconds later, Micah pressed his cockhead against Tyler's opening. His butt stretched farther with each of Micah's forward movements and the delicious pain blended with the pleasure as Micah sank deeper. Time drifted as Micah opened him. When Micah's pubes rubbed against his ass, Tyler sighed and fought to relax.

He panted as he experienced the sensation of Micah's thick cock inside him. Then Micah shifted and lightning shot through Tyler's body when Micah hit his prostate. "Oh, fuck, yes. There. Right there."

Micah gripped Tyler's waist and eased his cock almost out before plunging it deep inside Tyler. The maneuver had its desired effect.

"Fuck. Holy *fuck*," Tyler yelped.

After a few more thrusts, Tyler lost track of everything other than Micah pounding against that spot that brought him such pleasure. Micah's tight grip and cock thrusting inside him soon had Tyler roiling in pleasure. A few minutes later, they were moving in harmony and Tyler slammed back to meet each of Micah's thrusts.

Long minutes of exquisite pleasure filled Tyler then he felt Micah begin to tremble. With a final slam of his hips, Micah locked them together. Tyler moaned as Micah emptied his balls into him. Round after round flooded his gut as Micah's orgasm washed over them. Tyler enjoyed the wet, slick feeling of cum filling him as Micah's actions became less frantic. A few seconds later, Micah collapsed onto him.

"Damn. That felt amazing," Micah said.

Tyler slowly twisted under him, loving the sensation of cock and cum. Once they had both calmed, Micah eased Tyler on top of him until Tyler ground himself down on Micah. Tyler loved the feel of his husband's cock still inside him, as his climax built. Micah wrapped his hand around Tyler's cock and stroked him with maddening slowness while Tyler teased his nipples. The delicious sexual mix brought Tyler back to the edge. He began riding Micah's rehardened dick until his cockhead swelled red, hard and vein-covered.

With another few strokes, Tyler was overwhelmed with the familiar sensation of orgasm. His muscles clamped tight and the first strand of cum landed in front of them. With Micah buried deep inside him, it was the most mind-blowing sensation he'd had in some time. With a final seizing of his muscles, the last of Tyler's white cum oozed from the tip of his cock and over Micah's hand. With a last shudder of release, Tyler collapsed back into Micah's arms. After a minute, he twisted and gave Micah a kiss.

"That was amazing. *You* were amazing."

Micah gave him a tight embrace. "Ditto, lover boy. Ditto."

From that point, they held each other and whispered about their future together, with rounds of tender kisses as punctuation. Eventually though, the heat was almost gone and a few minutes later, Tyler untangled himself from Micah and moved to the edge of the bed.

"Hey," Micah said, "where are you going?"

Tyler smacked Micah on the bare ass and got a yelp for his effort. Then he said, "I'm showering before it gets too cold in here. Carl invited us to a ride this morning. If he says he's doing something, he will, but it'll be on his terms. Sometime he'll show up and want us ready to go."

He leaned down and gave Micah another kiss. "Come on. You can help me get the cum off."

Micah chuckled as he threw his legs over the bed and trotted after Tyler. As he ran past his new husband, he returned the smack on the ass. The two of them were still roughhousing when someone pounded at their door.

Tyler froze for an instant but then he heard, "You up yet? It's time for a ride."

Tyler rolled his eyes. "Well, fuck…"

Want to see more from this author?
Here's a taster for you to enjoy!

Leather and Grit:
Roping in his Heart
Jon Keys

Excerpt

Dakota groaned and shifted his position so the bright morning sunshine fell onto the bare body beside him. He lifted himself to his elbow and studied the pile of naked men spread across the bed he usually shared only with Ayden. The other two were buckle buddies they'd picked up the previous night. His guess would put them a good five years younger than either him or Ayden. They were college hustlers trolling for a cowboy to satisfy the itch they had for rodeo dick. One of them stretched and turned so his smooth, pale ass slid closer to Dakota. He extended his hand to caress the twink's butt. When the young man whined and wiggled nearer, Dakota decided one night with these two filled any kind of wild-oats-sowing he'd needed.

As he worked his way off the bed, the faint banging of pots and pans in use drifted into the bedroom. *Ayden. I should have guessed he'd make breakfast. He's always such a do-gooder.* Then the aroma of fresh coffee and frying bacon reached him, and Dakota's focus changed to the cooking odors he smelled. He swung his feet onto the plush hotel carpet. With clothes scattered across the room, he decided digging for underwear sounded like something he'd like to avoid. Certain the other two wouldn't be waking soon, he slipped into the living area buck naked.

He strolled across the white rug to stand in front of the floor-to-ceiling window and enjoy the warmth of the morning sunshine. A few seconds later, he stretched and tugged at his balls as he took in the sight of the giant steel-and-glass buildings surrounding him.

"You better watch who you're giving a show to. This isn't Vegas."

With a chuckle, Dakota slipped behind Ayden, drew him into a tight hug and kissed the side of his neck.

"Morning, babe. How are you? Did you enjoy yourself last night?" Dakota asked as he let his hands slip down Ayden's chest.

Ayden squirmed in his arms, chuckling as he grabbed Dakota's wrists and tugged him away. "Stop! You know how ticklish I am."

Dakota ran his fingers through the thick patch of hair surrounding Ayden's good bits then pulled his hands higher, exploring Ayden's chest before planting another kiss. Ayden laughed again as he dodged Dakota's embrace and went to the small refrigerator they'd stocked when they'd arrived. He waved Dakota toward the full pot of coffee as he checked the fridge. "The coffee's finished. Get some before our guests come out of their comas."

Dakota searched the kitchen cabinets, pulled out two white coffee mugs and poured them almost full. He stepped to the icebox and swatted Ayden's bare ass as his boyfriend picked out a few more things for breakfast.

Ayden snickered and glanced back at Dakota. "You better be careful or your sunny-side eggs will be well done."

Dakota put a few drops of half-and-half into his mug then finished filling Ayden's cup with cream and sugar. He set the swirling mixture beside Ayden, put his stout brew on the counter and hoisted himself up beside it. As he took his first sip, Ayden motioned in his direction. "You're kind of close to where I'm cooking. I'd hate to get bacon grease splattered on your family jewels. I don't know if you could go without sex long enough for it to heal."

Dakota studied Ayden while he took a drink of coffee, enjoying the warm sensation as it washed through his system. Once he'd swallowed, he refocused and blew Ayden a kiss. "You're the one with his willie a few inches from hot grease. Besides, if I get burns, you'll have to kiss them and make them all better."

"One of these days someone is going to get more attention than you," Ayden said with a laugh.

Dakota shook his head. "Nope, not going to happen." He stole a piece of crisp bacon from the platter and winked as he bit off the end.

Ayden laid another few pieces of thick bacon in the skillet to fry. Then he pushed a loaf of fresh sourdough toward Dakota and pointed to the knives along the tiled backsplash. "Make yourself useful and slice the bread."

"No problem, boss. But I'm telling you those two aren't going to be awake for at least a couple of hours."

Ayden waved a hand toward Dakota. "Just do it."

Dakota shrugged and carved the bread into Texas-size slices. Once he'd finished, there were several stacks of bread on the cutting board. He knew what Ayden had in mind and coated each slice with a generous amount of butter, first one side then the other. As Ayden cracked a half-dozen eggs into the sizzling hot bacon drippings, Dakota heated a sauté pan and laid slices of buttered bread on its hot surface. In a few minutes, he added a platter of buttered toast to the feast Ayden had created.

They seated themselves at the glass dining table and Dakota wiggled before grinning. "These chairs are gonna leave me with waffle butt."

Ayden studied Dakota's bare ass cheek through the glass and grinned. "True. You're going to have decorations, but it's still a fine ass."

About the time Dakota finished filling his plate, there was a crash, followed by a few select profanities from the bedroom. He lifted an eyebrow. "Sounds like our guests are up."

Another bang followed by a chorus of cursing drifted through the suite.

"Well, they're working on waking up at least."

Ayden pushed back his chair but Dakota stopped him. "They think they're adults. Let them figure out what to do."

Ayden drew his lips into a thin line but, after listening for a moment, he turned back to the meal. When Dakota snorted, Ayden paused halfway to his mouth with a fork filled with breakfast. "We don't want the food to get cold."

"That's it. I'm worried about the eggs getting cold. Yup, the eggs might get a chill."

Ayden paused and gave Dakota a glare, which turned into a grin. "Shut up or you can cook for the next month."

About the time Dakota had finished miming locking his lips and throwing away the key, the first of their overnight guests stumbled into the room. He mimicked a vampire's reaction when light hit them — at least the way they did in every bad vamp movie Dakota had ever seen. The college kid turned away, yanked up his jeans and buttoned them closed. When he turned back to the pair enjoying their quiet breakfast, he continued to shade his eyes from the morning sun.

"Fuck. Can't you close the damn curtain? It's too fucking sunny in here."

Dakota kept his typical smart-ass comments from coloring his next words as he pointed to the carafe filled with pitch-black liquid. "Ayden's made coffee. Grab yourself a cup if you'd like. There's breakfast on the counter too."

The pause stretched out while Dakota dug into his meal. Then he realized Ayden's chuckle had grown louder. He slowed to a stop and caught Ayden's scrutiny.

"What?" Dakota asked.

Ayden cut his eyes toward the half-clothed twenty-something. When Dakota followed Ayden's gaze, he saw the kid staring at Dakota's naked body. He let the exhibition go a little longer before calling him on it.

"See anything you like?"

"I think he's more ready for a breakfast sausage than thick-cut bacon," Ayden said.

"I see one thing I'd like to get more of," the college student said.

The last of the words had barely left his mouth when the other half of the pair stumbled in, tugging at the zipper on his jeans. He paused for a moment, taking in the scene. He curled his lips into a grin and winked at his friend. "Kev, why didn't you wake me?"

Kev had made his way to the kitchenette and filled his plate. As he shoveled food into his mouth, he wagged his fork. "I tried to get your fat ass up. You made weird noises and put the pillow over your head."

Ayden sighed and finished the last of the food on his plate. As he drained his coffee, he caught Dakota's eye. "I'll let the three of you enjoy the rest of breakfast. Eat whatever you want. Check-out time is ten."

Ayden took his dishes and put them on the kitchen counter, giving Dakota a chance to admire his hot body. When Dakota turned back, it was to glances that reminded him of hungry hens after a fat grasshopper. He had no desire to be the meal for these two, so he put his fork to use and enjoyed the last of his food. Once he'd taken care of his plate, he turned back to the pair, just in time to catch them with their eyes locked on his crotch. He decided a little teasing wouldn't be out of line. If they were going to stare, he'd give them something to remember.

He smirked as he studied them then seated himself on the counter. He eased his legs farther apart until his goods were displayed across the stone surface. Dakota decided that he'd sat on more comfortable things, but once he saw their faces, he was willing to tolerate some chill to drag these two into their own special brand of cowboy fantasy. They reminded Dakota of his dad's Blue Heelers begging for leftovers from the table. When he thought about it, they were after meat, the same as the pups. The similarity put a grin on his face.

"Last night was fun. Hope y'all enjoyed it as much as we did." Dakota teased the hair around his navel until they wiped sweat off their faces and licked their lips. Then he let his hand slip lower until he ran the tips of his fingers through his dark pubic hair. After a few minutes of teasing and when the two victims were seconds from popping in their pants, he stretched his tube of foreskin between his fingers, toyed with it for a moment then jumped to the floor. One of them moaned — Dakota didn't know which — but he had them at the level he'd wanted.

"Well, boys, I guess it's about time to clean up and get back to the rodeo. I'll catch up with Ayden. We'll see you in a bit." With a smile straight out of the legends of Coyote, he strolled from the room. By the time he reached the bedroom, the sounds coming from the living room left no doubt what was happening. He opened the door to find Ayden drying himself with a giant towel as thick as the carpet. As he dried between his legs, he glanced at Dakota with a smirk.

"Did you get them amped?"

Dakota put his finger to his lips, signaling Ayden to silence. It didn't take long for a symphony of moans and the slap of taut skin to fill the rooms. They listened for a few moments before Dakota grinned. "Sounds like something — or some*body* — got them all worked up."

Ayden tossed the towel into the bathroom, wrapped his fist around Dakota's cock and squeezed. "Oh yeah. I can't imagine what has them so excited." He released Dakota, aimed him toward the bathroom and swatted him on the butt. "Go wash off your crusty junk. By the time you're done, the two in the other room will be finished."

A guttural moan filled the suite.

"Or they may be done sooner. But get your ass in gear. We've spent enough time with this pair."

Dakota gave Ayden a tender kiss then strolled into the bathroom, making certain to work his butt so Ayden got a nice display. As he turned on the shower, he felt a presence in there with him. Dakota turned toward the door as he tested the temperature of the water with his hand. Ayden trailed into the shower behind him. With the spray from multiple heads hitting them from all sides, he ran his hands over the wet hair covering Dakota's chest. When Ayden dug his nails into Dakota's sensitive nipples, sparks of pleasure flooded his body.

He growled at Ayden. "You're getting something started."

"Which was my intent. It wasn't just the youngsters who got excited by the sight of your cock at breakfast."

"The calf roping doesn't start for hours. I wouldn't mind some fun before checkout."

Ayden sank to his knees and grabbed Dakota's butt before taking his hardening shaft between his lips. The heat of Ayden's mouth enveloped Dakota's dick as he took his boyfriend's hair in his hands and thrust. Ayden's tight throat drove Dakota toward his orgasm. The warm spray from a handful of shower nozzles only added to the experience.

"I'm close, and it's a big fucking load. You better pull off…"

When Ayden showed no sign of slowing, Dakota twisted his fingers through the wet ringlets covering Ayden's head and started a face fucking that left both of them groaning in appreciation.

The oh-so-familiar pleasure built in his crotch. As the intensity grew, Dakota's cock throbbed from Ayden's attention. It didn't take much before the first tidal wave of orgasm crashed over him. A low groan came from his lips as he unloaded into Ayden's throat. Once the last ripple of ecstasy had ebbed, Dakota helped Ayden to his feet and shared a scorching kiss. As he intertwined their tongues, Dakota enjoyed the delightful tastes. But as they held each other, Ayden's hard shaft slid across Dakota's stomach.

Without a word, Dakota squatted in front of Ayden and appreciated the sight before him. Ayden's dark brown hair was repeated in the groomed strip running between his pecs to the bush from which his rigid cock jutted. Dakota wrapped his hand around Ayden's dick and tugged back his ample foreskin. After a few slow strokes, he slid close and slipped his tongue into Ayden's hood.

The tastes and scents he found inside had become a favorite treat each time they made love. He explored Ayden's cock for several satisfying minutes before shifting his attention. He moved to the twin goose eggs Ayden carried for a set of balls. As he cradled them in his hand, Dakota pulled their sac lower until a bass rumble came from Ayden.

A few seconds later, Ayden groaned, "Damn, that's excellent. I love when you tease my balls."

Dakota sucked one in. As he coated it with spit, Ayden trembled and Dakota knew he had pushed too far.

"Ah, fuck. I'm coming!"

The shaking grew as Ayden grabbed Dakota's shorn head. A cry of pleasure marked the beginning of Ayden's climax. Dakota quickly swallowed Ayden's dick just as cum flooded his mouth until it dribbled from the corner. He took the last volleys and savored the bittersweet taste. When Ayden gave a final sigh, his softening cock slipped from between Dakota's lips.

He stood, held Ayden tight and gave him a lingering kiss before tugging them back under the warm spray. They rinsed and were soon using the last of the plush towels to dry themselves. As he slipped on a pair of deep red boxer briefs, voices from the other room drifted over to them. He glanced toward Ayden with a chuckle. "I think the bunnies are done. We need to get packed and back to the rodeo grounds."

Ayden nodded in agreement as he pulled clothes from the suitcase.

Sign up for our newsletter and find out about all our romance book releases, eBook sales and promotions, sneak peeks and FREE romance books!

About the Author

Jon Keys' earliest memories revolve around books; with the first ones he can recall reading himself being "The Warlord of Mars" and anything with Tarzan. (The local library wasn't particularly up to date.) But as puberty set in, he started sneaking his mother's romance magazines and added the world of romance and erotica to his mix of science fiction, fantasy, Native American, westerns and comic books.

A voracious reader for almost half a century, Jon has only recently begun creating his own flights of fiction for the entertainment of others. Born in the Southwest and now living in the Midwest, Jon has worked as a ranch hand, teacher, computer tech, roughneck, designer, retail clerk, welder, artist, and, yes, pool boy; with interests ranging from kayaking and hunting to painting and cooking, he draws from a wide range of life experiences to create written works that draw the reader in and wrap them in a good story.

Jon loves to hear from readers. You can find his contact information, website details and author profile page at https://www.pride-publishing.com